Mystery Lady

Striving to make a go of a village teashop after his previous career had come to an unscheduled halt, Paul Hunt seemed to be making fair progress—until a series of unwelcome events threw him off track.

Chief among them was his discovery of a murder. The victim was the Mystery Lady of Prior's Farm, who turned out to be something more than an old acquaintance, and while Paul was not exactly heartbroken by her demise, it certainly raised complications for him. Especially when the murder weapon was found in his vehicle, bearing his fingerprints.

Meanwhile, strange noises at his cottage were giving him sleepless nights, and to cap it all, his teashop was raided and vandalized, without apparent motive. Another puzzle hung over the sudden interest in the work of a young local artist whom Paul was trying to promote. Soon he was floundering in a morass of investigation that was finally to threaten his life and unveil the secrets surrounding the Mystery Lady.

by the same author

DUMMY RUN
HOUSE ARREST
THE SECOND TIME IS EASY
DEAD HEAT
PRIME TARGET
THE DARKER SIDE OF DEATH
CENSOR
A DOMESTIC AFFAIR
THE SEARCH FOR SARA
ALL PART OF THE SERVICE
RAINBLAST
BACKLASH
CATSPAW
DEATH FUSE
TOUCHDOWN
A DANGEROUS PLACE TO DWELL
DAYLIGHT ROBBERY
DIAL DEATH
MR T
DOUBLE DEAL
MURDER BY THE MILE
THE CLIENT
PHANTOM HOLIDAY
CRIME WAVE
DOUBLE HIT
CONCRETE EVIDENCE
ADVISORY SERVICE
DEADLINE
HUNT TO A KILL
DANGER MONEY
NO RETURN TICKET
NO THROUGH ROAD

MARTIN RUSSELL

Mystery Lady

THE CRIME CLUB
An Imprint of HarperCollins *Publishers*

First published in Great Britain in 1992
by The Crime Club, an imprint of
HarperCollins Publishers, 77–85 Fulham Palace Road,
Hammersmith, London W6 8JB

9 8 7 6 5 4 3 2 1

Martin Russell asserts the moral right to be identified
as the author of this work.

A catalogue record for this book is
available from the British Library

ISBN 0 00 232419 9

Photoset in Linotron Baskerville by
Rowland Phototypesetting Ltd
Bury St Edmunds, Suffolk
Printed and bound in Great Britain by
HarperCollins Book Manufacturing, Glasgow

FORETASTE

Stone walls.

These did a prison make. Huddled on straw, with my spine against a plank, I glared into the darkness and tried to remember how the rest of it went. Whoever was responsible for the lines, he had got it wrong.

Under certain conditions, the absence of light can be so total that conventional descriptions shed their meaning. This, beyond question, was such an occasion. The blackness nestled up against me: I could almost feel the nap of its surface. I wanted to retract my face, to withdraw, as though I were being nuzzled by some unwelcome inquisitive creature with whiskers.

The way to overcome this, I reasoned, was to look back. Calmly, examining each phase, relating one to the next, identifying pitfalls, plotting the detours that might have helped to cheat disaster. From this might arise a strategy for the immediate future. The lessons of history . . .

What this philosophy left out was the disagreeable fact that history seldom repeats itself in precisely the same way. Usually it has a trick or two up its sleeve. One had been played on me today already. Others might well lurk in the store chest.

One answer, perhaps, was to come up with a counter-surprise or two of my own. All that was required was to think of them.

I tried approaching things from a fresh slant. In this situation, what would an onlooker *expect* me to do? Claw at the stonework? Hurl myself at the door? Bellow and scream?

Now that my brain had stopped whirling, I was starting to be able to step into this other, mythical person's shoes, to observe myself from outside. It seemed a pace in the right direction. At the same time, apart from its mildly soothing effect, it produced little of tangible benefit. When all was said and done, flesh and bone were a poor match for timber and concrete. Many a wretch in many a dungeon had been forced to come to terms with this disheartening fact.

But I wasn't a wretch, for Heaven's sake. This was no dungeon. I was a civilized person who happened to find himself in a predicament that was going to demand a little time to resolve. That was all.

How much time had I got?

Like everything else, the watch on my left wrist was invisible. There was no means of gauging the duration of my stay to date. Certainly my mouth felt dry; this, however, could have been due to sheer funk as much as to liquid deprivation. Neither was I in the least hungry. Wrath and apprehension occupied the space where my appetite belonged.

In time, no doubt, hunger would crawl back. What was it like to starve to death?

To take my mind off the proposition, I abandoned lateral thinking in favour of a straightforward review of recent events. This proved easier. It had the merit, I told myself, of placing things in perspective as well as giving rise to the supply of possible aids to a solution. It was also a way of maintaining a grip on sanity. In the circumstances, this struck me as important.

CHAPTER 1

'Two coffees. One fruit scone.' I made a note of the order. 'That everything?'

Sally Ashby fell into reverie. 'The children will be along presently. Roger's showing them the deer in Coster's Wood. Perhaps a couple of Cokes?'

'I do a nice line in gassy lemonade.'

'Better not. They're bouncy enough as it is. Any more inflation and they'll float off to the coast. They're off home tomorrow. We shall miss them—at least I shall—but it'll give us a chance to scrape the bathroom free of its encrustation of carbolic soap and toothpaste.' She looked up at me with wide, trusting eyes. 'Why is it, Paul, that an ounce tube of Dentigel yields nine fluid kilograms of excess material? Is it some kind of Murphy's Law?'

'Myself,' I said, 'I use Buffshine. No waste products with that. It's so stiff, you need a kitchen mallet to hammer a wisp of it out of the nozzle.'

'Buffshine.' Finding an envelope in her bag, she jotted the name with a small gold pen. 'I'll try it. Might save our bacon next time. Talking of food, they'll probably be ravenous when they arrive. Bring doughnuts, will you? Roger will eat them, if they don't.'

'I thought you'd put him on a diet?'

'I have,' she said fondly. 'It's one of those where you're allowed rest days. You make up for it the following week.'

'How many can you have?'

'Doughnuts? Or rest days? I suppose it all depends on the calorie-count for any given period. Speaking for myself—'

'You're fine,' I told her, 'just as you are. And keep your voice down. You'll drive me out of business.'

'How's it doing, Paul?'

I pulled a face. 'I'm a quarter of the way through my first Five-Year Plan. That entails repayment of my father's interest-free loan. After that I'll concentrate on the mortgage. Taking the long-term view . . . I think I'm clinically insane. So cut it out, will you, about diets? I want everyone in this village eating and drinking their way to a cholesterol Paradise.'

'It's very naughty of you,' said Sally. 'But I do understand. Bring me a cheese scone, then, as well. I'm all for settling debt.'

I returned to the kitchen to transmit her order to Gillian, who was puce-cheeked over the range oven. 'I'm a bit behind with the scones, Mr Hunt,' she announced, pausing to refasten her mousy hair under its bright green headband and wipe her fingers with a length of tissue from the roller. 'Been having a spot of bother with the cooker. Got it now, though. Soon have the first batch. Them the only customers, so far?'

'It's a sharp morning,' I observed. 'Stand by for a stampede later.'

Clumping noises in the shop signalled the arrival of a number of bodies. ''Morning, Paul,' huffed Roger Ashby as I emerged. 'Not met Annie and Charles, have you? Only their second visit to these parts. Kids, this is an old mate of mine, Paul the Pastrycook Man—chuck him a smile, he likes that. But you still won't get any more jam in your doughnuts. Sally bagged a table?'

'You've got unlimited choice,' I said gloomily. I followed them through to the tea-room. Ashby, who since I knew him in London had ballooned into a contented cruiser-weight, arranged chairs for the children before squashing himself into a basket seat out of which he bulged on both flanks, in the manner of an immense cushion stuffed into a hamper. His wife leaned across to make adjustments to the neckwear of Charles, a seraphic five-year-old with straw hair encircling most of his face like a trapper's hat. His sister, seven, looked on with maternal gravity.

'Where are we going tomorrow?' Sally inquired, tickling his chin. 'Before you leave for home?'

'Flower Show.' Charles's grin broadened.

'That'll be a treat,' I said dutifully.

Sally cupped her mouth with a hand. 'Charles has this notion that it's some kind of puppet display.'

'Giant hollyhocks,' amplified her husband, 'dancing on wires, under attack from red-hot pokers . . . can't think how he picked up the idea.' He glanced innocently at Sally, who riposted with a look of indulgent reproach. 'See you there, Paul? Or are you keeping well clear?'

'Can't. In the first place, I'm providing the refreshments. And secondly, I'm ferrying the Sheeneys: their car's in the clinic again. So you'll see me around. Lots of luscious cream cakes,' I informed Annie, who remained deadpan while considering the news. 'Save a space after lunch, won't you?'

'What they favour,' remarked Ashby, 'are savoury niblets and that stuff you get heaving in plastic cartons with a built-in suction tube—constitution unknown, but the look of it reminds me of chocolate sago pudding. Perverted tastes, the young of today. Still, it does leave the delicacies for the rest of us. Here, Paul, you keep an ear to the ground. Anything fresh on the By-pass?'

'If you've heard nothing, I certainly haven't. Public inquiry still pending, I presume.'

He sniffed. 'Farce, that'll turn out to be. Half a million or so down the drain, just so that whatever the inspector decides can promptly be overruled by the relevant or irrelevant Minister in the name of democracy. What a country.'

'Roger,' his wife explained loyally, 'has his eye on that rather promising oasthouse facing Corkscrew Lane at the bottom—you know it? If the new road is going to wipe it off the map, it's obviously not a proposition. On the other hand . . .'

'If the road runs anywhere near, it could add to its value?'

'Something like that,' Ashby agreed cheerfully. 'Mark you, if the price were to drop low enough I might shove in an offer anyhow. We'll see. In the meantime, Paul . . .'

'What?'

'Should you happen to start thinking of jacking it in here, bear us in mind, won't you? I might be interested.'

'Paul's only had the place eighteen months,' Sally protested. 'And it was you recommended it to him in the first place.'

'Of course I did. Been regretting it ever since.'

'Well, give Paul a chance to make a go of it before you run him out of town.'

'Simply making my position known.' Ashby slipped me a wink. 'Getting to quite like it here, aren't you, my old son? Not a thoroughly bad lot, when you get to know us.'

'An interesting case study,' I assented.

'Who is?'

'The community at large. It's not that different from Highgate Village, with agriculture attached.'

'Ah. Dear old Highgate.' He gazed sentimentally into space. 'Had some rip-roaring times there, didn't we?'

'Did we?'

Sally delivered an affectionate prod to his waistline. 'Things always acquire a rosy glow for Roger in retrospect. You were perfectly happy, weren't you, darling, to move here and rusticate? Admit it.'

'Can't say I was too thrilled at the time. But I've grown into the role.'

'You certainly have. How about you, Paul? Do you miss the lights of London?'

'A bit like the survivors watching the *Titanic* go down.'

'Glad you're not on it, you mean?'

'Exactly.'

Ashby turned a brooding look upon me. 'You always struck me as a city type, actually. Gripped by the cesspool of society. Studying the cross-infection. I was fairly taken aback when we heard you wanted to get out.'

I shrugged. 'Tastes change. By the way, would you mind not referring to cesspools just now? It happens to be a sore topic.'

'Oh? How come?'

'Neighbour trouble,' I explained. 'My entire drainage system feeds into a tank in their garden. It tends to lead to problems.'

'Price you pay, old boy, for primitive existence. Thought you liked it in Parsons Lane?'

'Suits me nicely, otherwise.'

'But you wouldn't say no to a different cottage? Make you an offer for yours.'

'Roger, can't you forget property for three minutes? Paul doesn't want to sell.'

'How d'you know?'

'Ask him.'

'I just did.'

'You've enough on your plate already, I'd have thought. There's the oasthouse, and there's the Barn, not to mention the Manor . . . you can't go around putting in offers for all and sundry.'

'What's to stop me?'

Sally looked at me in despair. 'You'd think money had never been invented. Sellers are rather inclined to insist on payment, you know, before they hand over.'

Her husband gave me a nudge. 'You'd sign a cheque or two, my sweet, if I asked you.'

'Only to keep you out of jail.' She sat surveying him like a doting parent trying hard, and just failing, to seem severe.

'You'd never think,' she added in my direction, 'he was once an estate agent. Hopelessly impractical.'

'A prime qualification, I'd have said,' I remarked.

'Whose side are you on?' Ashby inquired without rancour. 'At least I had the wit to get out when I saw the danger signals. These days it's a buyer's market. I keep telling Sal, she should put some of that inheritance of hers to more active use, scatter it around into brick and tile— OK, prices have slumped, but they'll rebound. You can't hold the tide back. So, Paul, how about it? A cash offer, waste disposal included.'

'I like my pad,' I said mildly. 'I wasn't thinking of upping roots again. Not yet awhile.'

'I should say not!' Sally exclaimed. 'What should we do without the Pantiles? No basket chair comfort, no gossip, no stimulus. If you were to leave the neighbourhood—'

'Who said anything about Paul leaving the neighbourhood? He could keep things going here and live over the shop.'

'He likes his cottage.'

'Couple of goodish rooms overhead, as I recall. Tony Mansfield from Property Associates showed me over when I was half-thinking of investing in the place myself— before I contacted you, Paul, that was—and I was quite impressed. You could hive a bit of one room off for a bathroom and still have—'

'Roger, you're incorrigible. Ignore him, Paul. You're happy where you are. Living over the shop is for . . . prime ministers. You hang on to your Parsons Lane sanctuary.'

'I intend to.'

'Wait until they fix the line of the By-pass across your back garden: then see who's willing to buy you out.' Ashby beamed up at the entrance of Gillian with a tray. 'Look, Charles—doughnuts. Sugar-soaked and jam-infested. If you don't fancy it . . . He fancies it. Thanks, love,' he told

Gillian, who was lowering coffee cups hazardously past his left shoulder while breathing noisily into his ear. 'Still driving you hard, is he? Don't stand for any nonsense. Quote the Shop Acts at him if it all gets on top of you.'

Gillian, having achieved touchdown with the crockery, permitted herself a titter. 'He's all right reely, Mr Ashby. Not so bad when you get to know 'im.' She stood off to scan the table. 'Need any more cream, just holler.' She withdrew in crackles of denim and Polyester. Sally pursued her departure with an expression of kindly interest.

'Nice child. You were lucky, Paul, to get hold of her. They wanted her in the supermarket, didn't they?'

'So rumour has it. I'm well aware of my luck. She takes over whenever I want her to. I can't imagine what I'd do without her.'

'Keep her sweet, then,' Ashby counselled, biting into a scone. 'False economy, underpaying your staff. As an ex-finance man, Paul, you should be aware of that.'

'I'm sure Paul needs no lessons in staff relations,' murmured his wife, stretching across to remove red jam from the chin of Charles. 'Annie, keep an eye on your brother —he's going to tread doughnut into the carpet if we don't watch out.'

The girl giggled. 'OK, Auntie Sal.'

'And talking of relationships, Paul, have you managed to establish any with your new neighbour?'

'My new . . . ?'

'The Mystery Lady. The one who's taken over Prior's Farm.'

'Oh. Her. Hardly a neighbour,' I pointed out. 'That spread is half a mile along the lane from me.'

'In these parts, that's next door. Have you met her?'

'I'd only vaguely heard there was anybody there. How long has she had the place?'

Sally consulted her husband. 'About a month, isn't it, darling? Isn't that what Tony Mansfield told you?'

Ashby munched through a mouthful of scone before replying. 'Is it? Don't recall. Rarely go that way, myself. But you're well in her ambit, old son. A rogue male on the prowl. Why don't you make contact? Offer to cater for her house-warming.'

'Who says she's having one? Anyway, she's probably ninety.'

'Just what I said to Sal. Made no difference, though . . . she's still consumed with curiosity, like the rest of the female population. It only needs—'

'You've got to admit,' interceded his wife, 'she's a Challenge. Nobody seems to know a thing about her.'

'Why should they?'

'I mean, there she is, all alone apparently in that rambling old semi-ruin, surrounded by fifty acres of scrub, keeping herself to herself: naturally we're curious. What's she doing there? Does she plan to farm?'

'Why don't you call on her?' I suggested. 'Woman to woman. You'd have her life history in six minutes flat.'

Ashby flipped an eyebrow at me. 'As long as that?'

His wife sighed. 'Polly Newbold has tried already. Couldn't get a reply.'

'If the Rector's wife can't break through, what hope for the rest of us?' Collecting crumbs into a mound on his plate, Ashby scooped them up with a teaspoon and conveyed them with enjoyment to his mouth. 'The reason she got no answer is probably that the doorbell's on the blink. Can't imagine anything working in that dump.'

'Is the place that derelict?'

'Roger made a bid for it once. But when he saw the work it would have needed . . .'

'*Work?* It wanted ninety pounds of Semtex and a fresh

start. The Brookers just let it fall into decay. When they refused to drop the price, I lost interest.'

'The Mystery Lady was willing to take it on, though, it seems. Unless she's renting.'

'In which case,' I said, 'she obviously wants to be left alone. So I'll do her a favour and respect her wishes.'

Later that morning, I was selling a chocolate sponge to a wizened resident of the sheltered flats on the other side of the main street when the shop doorbell chimed to admit a girl clutching a leather case of giant expanse. I spared her a quick smile.

'With you in a sec, Sandra. Anything else, Mrs Guttridge? We're out of fairy cakes, I'm afraid. All earmarked for the Flower Show.'

'Don't want no fairy cakes. Give us indigestion last time. What you put in 'em, too much soda or summat?'

'Maybe too little,' I said jocularly. 'Tell you what. Gillian's made some nice parkins, treacly, the way you like 'em. Try a couple of those? You'll enjoy them for tea. How's the grandchild?'

She gave me a sidelong bloodshot look. 'Messed us all up, he did, yesterday. Looked after him while his mum went along to the clinic. Took us an hour after he'd gorn, it did, tidying the rooms.'

'But you wouldn't have him any other way,' I admonished, stuffing paper bags into her carrier and wrenching from her claw a five-pound note that appeared to have been used to wrap a damp sausage. Having scrutinized her change, she retreated to the door, stood holding it ajar.

'Don't you go having no youngsters of yer own,' she advised the waiting girl. 'More trouble'n they're good fer.'

'You don't mean that, Mrs Guttridge.'

'Don' I?' She departed cackling. The girl and I exchanged looks, and then laughs. I reached out a hand for
the leather case.

'Something for me?'

'Not sure if it's any good,' she said defensively. Unzip-
ping the càse, she extracted a framed picture which she
passed over. Propping it against the side of the till, I stood
back for an appraisal.

'It's good. Let me see . . . The Horse and Hound at
Fetchmere?'

'Right.' She cheered up. 'What do you think?'

'I think I've just the right spot for it. Come through.'

She followed me into the tea-room, depopulated after a
mid-morning minor surge. I held the picture against the
white-emulsioned wall behind the table for six inside the
recess that had once been a vast inglenook. 'With the light
on—' I threw the switch—'it stands out nicely. Price?'

'It's there, in the corner.'

I peered. 'Forty-five quid. OK. Giving it away, in my
view, but it's your decision. Hang it there, shall we?'

'Super. Thanks. I thought even forty-five,' she added
diffidently, 'was a bit of a cheek, considering the other three
haven't sold.'

'They will,' I said heartily. Our gazes slid to the other
samples of her work occupying the space available each
side of the window commanding the main street. 'Purely a
matter of the right buyer coming in at the right time.'

'When he has his cheque-book with him, you mean?'

'I still think you should up the prices into the hundreds.
The psycho factor.'

Sandra said nervously, 'They might think they were getting something special.'

'They would be.'

'Let's stick to the forties for the moment. If I flogged one
at that price I'd be over the moon. Thanks, Mr Hunt. I

won't swing another one on you till one of these has gone,
I promise.'

'They give the place a tone,' I assured her. 'Only wish
I'd more space. How's your brother?'

'Not too bad.' Her eyelids performed the rapid flutter
that betokened, I had come to realize, a form of camouflage.
'Fastened his own shirt buttons this morning. Most of them.
Mind you, it took him an hour.'

'He'll be decorating the studio next. Still zipping around
on that moped of yours?'

'Couldn't manage without it.' She refastened the case.
'You know where I am, Mr Hunt, in case anyone—'

'I'll be on the blower the moment it happens. It's Paul,
by the way.'

She looked baffled. 'What is?'

'The first of the four-letter words that constitute my title.'

'Oh. Right. I'll . . . be seeing you, then,' she said bash-
fully, sweeping her blonde hair back. She paused by the
counter. 'Could I have some marshmallows?'

'You don't have to, you know.'

'They're for John. He really goes for them.'

Taking her money, I said, 'If I ever lose Gillian—God
forbid—I'll need somebody to replace her. How would you
fancy life over a hot range?'

She smiled, shook her head. 'Couldn't leave John.'

'You could dodge home several times a day.'

'I'll carry on as I am, thanks. Painting's more my line.'

'You never spoke a truer word,' I agreed. 'One day soon,
somebody's going to wake up to the fact.'

CHAPTER 2

For as long as anyone could remember, what was loosely termed the Spring Flower Show had taken place on the terraced lawns of Appleby House at the southern edge of the village, by kind permission of the owners, Colonel and Mrs Wallis, who also donated the hire of the marquee.

In truth, the function had little to do with anything of a floral nature, since it occurred at a time of the year remarkable chiefly for the striped tulips cultivated, as part of a long tradition, by the Appleby House gardener, Percy Carter, who it was widely felt should not be deprived of a showcase for his efforts. Beyond this, the horticultural contributions were a minor feature of the event. Homemade produce by the Women's Institute and artistic creations from the local school made up the balance, and even then the amount of exhibition space available under canvas was somewhat in excess of demand. Over the years, the Colonel and his lady had formulated a system of spacious display which masked the situation, although nobody was fooled. What people went along for were the sideshows, the sporting fixtures, the teas and the gossip. Flowers, fruit and vegetables could await the Autumn Show in October, where they belonged.

The magnificence of the venue was in violent contrast to the habitation of my nearest neighbours but one, for whom on this occasion I was acting as chauffeur. Bridget and Patrick Sheeney, a sturdy couple in their eighties, had much in common with the house that partly sheltered them: Timbers, an edifice of crumbling stone and rotting oak which stood—with some uncertainty—on the fringe of woodland just around the bend from my own cottage in Parsons Lane.

They, too, were tottering but indestructible. Our relationship had started off on a similar footing. My initial gaffe had been to induce involuntary abortions among their hens by reversing my elderly Land-Rover in unwise proximity to their quarters; although either of them was capable of wringing any number of the birds' necks without a pang when occasion demanded, up to that point they were sentimental about the creatures, addressing each of them by name and fiercely protective of their comforts. Acts of contrition on my part had rescued the situation. Now fast friends, we operated a system of mutual aid: I gave them lifts when they were stranded and about once a fortnight, in return, I went to Timbers for lunch.

They were stranded not infrequently. The metal fatigue that had begun to afflict their battered estate car, of dubious brand and vintage, was fast developing into a kind of automobilized motor neurone disease requiring sustained and increasingly regular spells of treatment at the village clinic for clapped-out conveyances. During its brief interludes of semi-revival, Bridget was the driver. Her husband, who had been reared in Southern Ireland at a time when the concept of internal combustion was roughly on a level with that of flying saucers, was apt to propel a motor vehicle on the public highway in much the same way as he had once driven tractors over hillsides. 'Patty,' his wife was fond of observing, 'has about as much road sense as Reggie, and his eyesight isn't so good.' Reggie, their dizzy Springer spaniel, was released each morning to roam the district and owed his continued existence to the forbearance of the local traffic, which had learned to cope with his vagaries.

Bridget herself, who tended to favour changing to a higher gear rather than a lower one for corners, and advanced out of road junctions on the principle that any contraflow vehicles must take such evasive action as seemed called for at the time, was scarcely in a position to pass

judgement; but what might have been insupportable in anyone else was, in a perplexing way, part of her charm. There
was no side to either of them. Most people took them as
they were: warm-hearted, outgoing, hugely entertaining,
tough as farm boots. If there was a funny side to something,
they saw it; if not, they invented it. Parsons Lane without
them was unimaginable.

Spot on cue for the Flower Show, their car had fallen
sick again, which was the reason they were sharing my
Land-Rover with six trays of mixed pastries to add to those
I had already supplied for allocation by the Refreshments
Committee. When we arrived, the fancy dress parade was
in its closing stages and the sack race had just concluded
in a medley of limbs and coarse material on the third terrace
down. Old buddies of the Colonel and his wife, Bridget and
Patty were sucked instantly into their group by the marquee
entrance. I made off to deliver the eatables to the redoubt
of trestle tables guarding the western flank of the house,
manned by WI volunteers under their organizer, Miss
Clemfold, who fell upon me with dental gratitude.

'Just in the nick of time, Mr Hunt! There's been a run
on the rock cakes. A positive run. Do you have any more?'

'Luckily,' I said, 'Gillian guessed they might be popular,
so she came up with another batch. She has a flair.'

'These look scrumptious. And coffee eclairs. You mustn't
leave us, Mr Hunt. Don't give up the Pantiles, will you?
Promise?'

'Did somebody say I was planning to?

Miss Clemfold went a light shade of pink. 'Not to my
knowledge. But some people have itchy feet these days,
don't you find? No sooner installed somewhere than they're
off somewhere else.'

'Not me. I'm the inert type.'

'That *is* good news. Have some tea.'

Brushing my lips with the acidic wash that she provided

from a pot the size of a camellia tub, I stood aside from the ruck to observe the scene. The group that had claimed the Sheeneys now included the Rector, the Rev. Edgar Newbold, and his wife Polly, an earthy couple with few illusions pertaining to human frailty, a condition to which they themselves were not immune. For reasons not exclusively evangelical, the Rector was a valued customer at the Stag, the largest of the three hostelries in the village main street, where he conducted the equivalent of an MP's surgery five nights a week; while Polly, who smoked untipped cigarettes with the abandon of one who had never heard of the anti-tobacco lobby and would have hooted in its face if she had, was the unabashed focal point for any gossip or slander that might be doing the rounds. Despite or because of these traits, they were a likeable pair. Curious to discover what was creating so much mirth, I surreptitiously disposed of my cup and started out towards them. Prior to arrival I was waylaid.

'Paul, dear. Just a quick word. I'm afraid the tank wants emptying again.'

Holding my features in check, I moulded them carefully into a forgiving smile of resignation before turning them upon Myrtle, my immediate neighbour in Parsons Lane. 'Already? Surely it's just a few weeks since—'

'I *know*. Isn't it shocking? But Don lifted the cover yesterday and had a look, and it's well up. *Well* up. So we thought we'd better give you early notice, in case they're behind with the service. You never can tell.'

'I'll drop an order into the post. Can't have your borders covered in sludge, can we?'

She gave a theatrical shudder. 'I can't tell you, Paul, what a relief it is to have someone *reasonable* to deal with. The Fishers never bothered. We could mention it in March, and by June we'd have to ask them again, and still they forgot about it. Since you came, we've been spared that.'

'Happy to oblige.'

'But it's a constant nuisance, I must say. The blessed thing seems to fill so fast.'

'I must remember to go easy on baths.'

Myrtle, who resembled her husband in being pudgy, limp-haired and slightly cross-eyed, took the remark as seriously as she treated everything else. 'A couple of inches can make a lot of difference, no question of that. Say you have three baths a week: Don says if you normally use twenty gallons, a reduction of—'

'OK, Myrtle, I'll send the order off tomorrow. Have you and Don anything in the show?'

She blinked. 'Rather soon in the year for us. Don did have some nice tulips which he was thinking of entering, but we decided that might seem like a bit of a dig at old Percy—tulips are his thing, aren't they?—so we left it. How about you? Any Highly Commendeds for your home-made cakes?'

'If there were, they'd have to go to Gillian. She's the powerhouse of the operation.'

'She went to catering college, you know.'

'Yes, she told me.'

'I wonder why she never got on.'

'Got on?'

'Took over, I mean, in a big establishment. Made more use of her qualifications.'

'Instead of languishing with a one-man outfit in a Hampshire village? You might ask her some time.'

'I will. Next time I'm in for morning coffee. That'll be next Thursday. Tuesday I'm helping out with the playgroup, and Wednesday—'

'Someone's beckoning to me,' I lied. 'You'll have to excuse me, Myrtle. Try your luck on the tombola over there. You might win a week in a cesspool-free zone.'

Leaving her with a blank expression, I joined the group

near the marquee. 'What's the joke?' I demanded of Bridget, who was brick-red in the face, her immense and jutting teeth gleaming like a trail of white ash in a log fire. She planted a powerful hand on my shoulder, causing me to buckle at the knees.

'Bernard,' she spluttered, 'ordered a medium-sized tent with an awning, thirty display units and half a dozen portable loos. Phwat did he get?' Her laughter boomed out across the garden. 'A Jumbo Big Top with an anteroom, ten reinforced stands for performing lions, and no lavatories. This was yesterday.'

'Good Lord.'

'And when they turned up this morning with the replacement, someone had forgotten to load the main uprights on to the lorry. So at seven a.m. there they were, frantically telephoning . . .' Bridget's utterance vanished under pressure.

The Colonel took over. 'What it boils down to, Paul, is that this mass of canvas over our heads is slung on a couple of telephone poles we scrounged from the heap that's been lying on the verge in Lovers' Walk for the best part of six months. We reckoned nobody would miss 'em.'

'Fair bet.'

'Oh, but they did. Just had someone on from BT, wanting to know what the Hell, etcetera. I said they could have their poles back when we've done with 'em. They're claiming compensation . . . I think. Negotiations continue.'

'Keep your end up, Colonel. Brazen it out.'

'In the meantime, both toilets in the house are at full stretch and we've got the first eight-foot performing pyramid of spring blooms in living memory stacked on steel jump-stools at the centre of operations . . . pop inside, my boy, and take a look. At least we've managed to save Percy's face. That's what counts. Oh, before you rush off. Most grateful for the provisions. Well up to snuff. Many thanks. Settle up in due course.'

'Get your profits in first.'

'Isn't he a treasure?' Bridget embraced me with a well-filled sleeve. 'No mercenary instincts. Patty and I are just off to sample the merchandise. Anything with chocolate? We skipped· lunch to leave room for the goodies. That is, we cut out the dessert. Seen the Mystery Lady yet?'

'Is she here?'

'I've not the least idea.' Bridget aimed a demonic grin. 'We did think you might have succeeded in luring her along. But then, you're probably too taken up with the other young madam, the budding artist—Brenda? Wanda? *Sandra*. Talented little thing. Shame about her brother.'

'Rotten luck,' I agreed.

'MS, is it? I thought so. Plucky of her to take him on.'

'Apparently she's the only family he's got. Their parents split up a few years ago, and the mother's since died and the father's remarried and gone to live in Nairobi or somewhere hot. Sandra really hadn't much choice.'

'How old is she?'

'Early twenties, I think. Her brother's older.'

'Does he get an attendance allowance?'

'I believe so, plus a bit of help from the society. Sandra was hoping to supplement that from her pictures.'

Bridget regarded me severely. 'Her brother can't be left, surely? How can she go out painting?'

'She doesn't. She scoots around on her moped, taking photos of likely subjects—she invested in one of these hi-tech cameras that do it all for you, telephoto lens, the lot. Then she works from the colour prints in the studio.'

'Where's the studio?'

'Up in their attic. Those cottages off the main street have all got these big dormer spaces with north-facing windows.'

'You've seen it, I suppose?' Bridget said innocently.

'Nice try, Mrs Sheeney—but no, I haven't. Sandra described it to me when I became her unofficial gallery owner. And in reply to your earlier question, you'll find some chocolate-coated shortbread on the tea tables, if it hasn't all been snapped up at bargain prices; if it has, I can recommend the Victoria sponge. I'm off to view the tulips.'

On my way into the marquee I barged somebody's shoulder. 'My fault,' I apologized. 'Did I hurt you?'

'I'm used to worse.' The young woman I had pitched off balance adjusted her grip on the string bag she was holding; it bulged with what looked like an assortment of Gillian's morning output. 'No harm done,' she added, turning to resume her original course for the car park. I had a swift impression of dark, deepset eyes under a mantle of hair that was neither tawny nor raven while containing elements of both, like a skilful weave of rug. Although not tall, she was slender and had an uprightness of carriage that added to her stature. There was a resolute action to her walk. As I was gazing after her, the Rector approached with a look of some amusement.

'Been given the brush-off, Paul?'

'I'm not sure. Who is she, Edgar, do you know? Not the enigma from Prior's Farm, by any chance?'

The amusement changed to surprise. 'That's Angela, our revered new schoolteacher. She's been here three weeks. Thought you'd have run up against her by now.'

'I just did, rather heavily. Taken over, has she, at the church school? What became of Miss Somerby?'

'Hounded into early retirement by the mini-mob. Well, basically it was chronic asthma. Angela came to us with golden references. She was at the primary school in Bobdean for a couple of years, and she also gave private tuition. I must say, the kids seem to eat out of her hand.'

'Literally, I should think. She was carrying about half a

hundredweight of Pantiles produce. From the size of her, it's not meant for herself.'

The Rector nodded profoundly. 'Bribe material, I imagine. Not that she needs it. I'm surprised you didn't seize your chance.'

'My chance?'

'To shoulder the burden for her. Ideal way to get acquainted.'

'I wasn't angling for an introduction. Just inquisitive.'

'Same as the rest of us. Prior's Farm, I'm talking about. Now there's a riddle. Still no sighting of the lady, it seems, since she moved in. Most odd.'

I looked at him cynically. 'If the neighbourhood at large is so keen to get to know her, surely you of all people—'

'Oh, Polly's had a bash, don't you worry. Several sorties. Each time she's gone along, though, there's been no answer to her knocks and not a sign of life around the farmhouse. She doesn't appear to be on the phone. It's driving Polly crackers.'

'Maybe the Dark Lady just likes her privacy.'

'If it's seclusion she's after,' said the Rector in all seriousness, 'she should know better than to move into an isolated rural property all by herself. Simply screaming for attention.'

I nodded with equivalent gravity. 'Epic miscalculation. What she should have gone for was a glass-walled apartment in Piccadilly Circus. No sign of life, you say? No vehicle?'

'Yes. A small hatchback. Fiat, I believe. Parked round the back, with its doors locked. Polly tried them,' he explained without embarrassment. 'If she could have got inside, she'd have sounded the hooter.'

'And the house itself? All locked and barred?'

'Even the downstairs curtains were drawn across the windows. Polly couldn't see through.'

'Frustration,' I murmured, 'can bite no deeper. She must venture out now and then, this recluse. She'd need supplies.'

The Rector gestured. 'Unless she moved in with a car-load. But no amount of stuff lasts indefinitely.' He stood gazing absently at the tug-of-war in progress on the lawn below us, before twitching himself back into priestly mode. 'A tormented soul, no doubt,' he said piously, 'seeking peace or redemption. Who are we to deny it her? The thing that concerns me is that she may be in need of help.'

'If so, she'll ask for it.'

'People don't always, you know.'

'In which case, there's not much to be done.'

'There's always something one can do. However, I will admit she's doing her best to make it difficult. *Should* you catch a glimpse of her, Paul, do find out all you can, won't you? Polly will be so grateful.'

I gave him a solemn pledge. Detaching myself, I escaped into the marquee, avoiding the onset of a chill April down-pour which had been threatening for some time. Inside, Percy Carter's tulips were starting to wilt. The most impressive display was on the Home Cookery section, where the Rector's wife, I noticed, had distinguished herself by taking two Firsts and a Third with her raisin rockcakes, vanilla fudge and apple flan, all thrown off presumably in the brief intervals between expeditions to Prior's Farm. Bridget had earned a Commended for a dish of cindery fragments described on the docket as Country-Style Melt-ing Moments. The sole reason for the award appeared to be that no other comparable confection had been submitted for judging. Pleased for her, I returned across squelching grass to the refreshment tables to convey the news.

The Sheeneys, hands clasped about beakers of tea and paper plates slowly disintegrating under the combined stresses of food and rainwater, were in lively debate with

the helpers, who were doing their best to protect the delicacies with umbrellas. 'Commended?' trumpeted Bridget
in mock disgust. 'Phwat sort of reward is that for two hours
crouched over a hot cooker? Catch me entering again! Anything I make in future can go towards the horses. May the
seventh, Paul. Make a note in your diary.'

'It's noted.'

'Can we count on you to sell the raffle tickets at the door?
You were a whizz at it last year.'

Resignedly I gave my word. Annually, Bridget held a
home bring-and-buy sale to raise funds for a pony sanctuary
in Wales. If the previous year's event had been typical, I
was in for another morning of unmitigated chaos. 'What
are the raffle prizes this time?' I demanded. 'Last year, the
exercise bike went to Miss Higgins at the Ivy Nursing
Home, just in time for her ninety-eighth birthday. Can't we
arrange things better than that?'

'The matron,' Bridget replied with dignity, 'has had a
lot of good use out of it. Anyway, first prize this year is a
garden fork.'

'Oh, great. Miss Higgins had better stand by: it'll just
be in time for her ninety-ninth. Next year, a squash rac-
quet? She'll need more than a telegram from Buckingham
Palace after forty minutes on court at the Leisure Centre.
Tell you what,' I added, on an inspiration, 'why not invite
the Mystery Lady from Prior's Farm to come along and
man a stall? She may be another equine fanatic.'

'Phwat a good idea! But how do I get in touch?'

'Shove an invite through her door.'

'You can do that for me, Paul. It was your idea. Come
to lunch tomorrow and I'll give you a note to take along. I
wouldn't eat that, Patty, it's gone gungy at the edges. Come
along, I want to see the awards.'

'Are you OK for a lift back?'

'The Ashbys have kindly promised to take us.'

'In their Vauxhall Carlton,' Patty informed me, his eyes shining like a schoolgirl's.

'After the outward trip, you deserve a spot of luxury. See you tomorrow, then. Usual time.'

I made my way back to the car park. Puddles were forming in the least avoidable places. Splashing through some of them to the Land-Rover, I paused at sight of the schoolteacher, the dark-eyed Angela, peering beneath the opened bonnet of a middle-aged Renault 5 a few vehicles away. 'Need a hand?'

'No, thanks.' She let the bonnet drop with a clash. 'Just drying out the leads.' Wiping her fingers on a yellow duster, she got into the car and touched the motor to life; it had an efficient, schoolmistressy throb to it. Backing sinuously out, she sped to the exit. By the time I reached the same point, the Renault was out of sight.

'How'd it go, then, Mr Hunt? What they think of the scones an' that?'

'The scones went like . . . hot scones. You're a culinary legend in the district, Gill, did you know? You should publish a book of recipes.'

'I did,' she said startlingly. '*Things To Do With Herbs and Spices*. Mortleys printed it for us.'

'I'd no idea. Congratulations. Sell many?'

'Thirty-eight,' she said with pride. 'The money went to Spastics.'

'Well done. Thanks for holding the fort this afternoon. Any problems?'

Gillian considered. 'Old Mrs Guttridge came in to say she broke a tooth on one of them parkins you sold her yesterday.'

'She hasn't got any teeth.'

'A bit of her dentures, then. Quite upset, she was. Said she'd be back again in the morning.'

I sighed. 'She'll be after a complimentary pack of marsh-mallows. She can cope with those, she keeps telling me. Anything else?'

'Creepie Felrose popped over from opposite.'

'What was he after?'

'Never said. When he found you wasn't here, he said it didn't matter and he'd try again later.'

'Don't fancy the sound of that.' Through the shop window, I peered across the main street at the glazed front-age on the other side; shielding a rabble of furniture and artefacts, it was topped by mint-green lettering announcing THE LUCKY DIP. ANTIQUES, LIGHT REFRESHMENTS. FREE ADVICE, VALUATIONS. BROWSERS WELCOME. 'Something's needled him,' I muttered. 'Have I offended him lately? Besides opening up here in the first place, I mean.'

'Huh. Don't need to do nothing to put his nose out of joint. Slit the throat of his own grandmother, he would, if she took her custom somewhere else.'

'Can I help it if we've pinched trade from his horrible little dainty teas on fake Jacobean tables with bogus Geor-gian cutlery? He should have made an offer for you before I got in first.'

Gillian shuddered. 'Catch me working for 'im. Gives me the shivers, just seeing 'im at a distance.'

'Better take cover, then. Here he comes again.'

With a squeal, Gillian ran for the shelter of the kitchen and shut herself in. Moments later, Lionel Felrose minced into the shop. He was wearing his tartan cap. The reason for this was not the rain, which had stopped, but his almost total cranial nudity: he kept his head covered at all times, indoors or out, and had even been known to affront the Rector by refusing to expose his scalp at morning service, claiming a skin rash. The rest of him, of which there was a meagre amount, was encased in a short velvet jacket above tight slacks of a curious orange tint which made him appear to be walking on long, tapering sticks of iced lolly. It disturbed me to note that I was being granted a spacious view of his stained and irregular front teeth, a sign of ebullience that I had learned to distrust.

'*Hallo*, Paul. Just disposed of a rather marvellous little Spode vase that came from Whitton's Oast—you know, where the Smythes are moving out. Fetched the asking price. Collector from Hindlebury.'

'Good for you, Lionel.'

'So I thought I'd prance over for a few slim panatellas to celebrate. Yes, one of those packets of five. You don't, do you, yourself? I thought not. And a box of matches. You *do* sell everything, don't you?'

'Gill tells me you came across earlier.'

'I'd *totally forgotten* you were feeding the five thousand. Sooner you than me, dear boy, to be entirely truthful. My mass catering days are behind me, I'm relieved to say. *Much* happier purveying the odd savoury nibble and glass of wine to the occasional serious client who finds his way into the showroom.' Turning to the window, Lionel stood for a moment admiring his shopfront before spinning again. 'Paul, you can help me. At least I'm hoping you can. This new arrival in the district, I gather she's a near neighbour of yours, am I right? Prior's Farm. You wouldn't just happen to have—'

'That's right, Lionel, I wouldn't. I'm afraid I know nothing about the lady. You're not the first person to ask.'

'Is that a fact? The reason I was inquiring—'

'You're wondering if she might have brought some family heirlooms with her?'

'Naughty Paul,' he said, wagging a finger. 'But of course you're absolutely on the button. These hard times, one can't afford to ignore the slightest . . . What I had in mind was to sound her out, tactfully you know, not pushing her in any way: but I don't know, she seems frightfully hard to make contact with. She's ex-directory, and she hasn't replied to the card I sent her a week or two back. Then I thought of you.'

'I'm touched, Lionel.'

'Well, I remembered you live in Parsons Lane and it occurred to me—'

'I don't have much time or energy, you know, for paying social calls. When I get home, I tend to flake out.'

'Ooh, I *know* how it is.'

'Until people started asking, I'd hardly realized this newcomer was around. There's just one thing I might do for you.'

He cocked an avid head, like a sparrow on a bird table.

'I'm supposed to be delivering something to her from Bridget Sheeney. If you like, I can include another reminder for you. That help?'

'Paul, you're a *gem*. That would be marvellous. And should you chance to see the lady in the flesh, so to speak—'

'From all accounts, it's not likely. But I'll keep it in mind. That's three quid and tenpence, by the way.'

'Goodness me. What *am* I thinking of?' Returning from the door, he extricated a slim purse from a pocket of his trousers and paid the required sum meticulously on to the counter. 'You do have a living to make, Paul, don't you? Same as the rest of us. Righty-ho, then. I'll drop a bit of literature in tomorrow, for you to take along. What's the lady's name, by the by?'

'I've no idea.'

'*Never* mind. I'll have to address it to The Occupier again. Awfully obliged, dear boy. Carry on with the good work.'

'What did he mean by that?' queried Gillian, emerging from her retreat as the shop doorbell proclaimed his departure.

'I think he meant, Please drop dead in your tracks from

overwork. Which reminds me, Gill, it's time you were off. I'll close up.'

'Right you are, Mr Hunt.' Removing her coat from its hook, she paused in the act of wriggling into it. 'Glad I don't work for that slimy little toad,' she remarked. 'He'd be dead inside a week. Bashed over the bonce with his own fire-irons.'

CHAPTER 3

Lunch at Bridget's was a hazardous business. Apart from the meal itself, the edibility of which was governed by the vagaries both of cook and cooker—their ages were roughly parallel—there was always a risk of hypothermia. We were having a cold April. Timbers was in no shape to lessen its discomforts.

As the wife of an ex-farmer, Bridget permitted herself no indulgences such as packaged goods from the supermarket. Everything had to be home-reared, self-produced, incinerated nearly to destruction. After Bridget had done with them, little except pulp remained of the garden-grown frozen vegetables, while the roast duckling—one of a flock raised and throttled by Patty, who was in the habit of alluding to them fondly by name prior to murdering them—was frequently indistinguishable from the charred flesh of any other species. This did not prevent due ritual being observed. As nominal master of the house, Patty was allowed to perform the carving, a ceremony which usually culminated in the arrival upon each plate of a mound of chippings so minute that on one occasion I had mistaken it for chopped bay-leaf and had come within an ace of wounding my hostess's feelings beyond repair by gently reminding her that I was still awaiting my portion.

Wised-up by experience, I now directed energetic stirring movements at anything placed before me, rotated my jaws for twenty minutes in a parody of enjoyment, and ate when I got home.

Another of Patty's tasks was the replenishment of the open log fire which pretended to heat the ramshackle living-room, a low-beamed, groaning, shuddering, gale-tossed area wedged between kitchen and outhouse, furnished with a range of armchairs and spring-loaded sofas that seemed to have been salvaged from the local tip, and depending for its illumination upon a window the size of a tea-tray and a couple of forty-watt bulbs hidden in alcoves at opposite corners. The best place to be, I had discovered, was the kitchen, which managed to achieve roaring if fitfully high temperatures during the cremation process. Entering this sanctuary on the day after the Flower Show, I found a flushed and glistening Bridget agitating something languidly in a saucepan on the hob while conducting a bellowed conversation with someone out of view. She broke off to greet me with a smile hewn straight out of the chalk face.

'Go through, Paul. Patty will get you a drink. Lunch is a little held up, I'm afraid. We had a small disaster.'

'How small?'

'Reggie got hold of the duck.' The kitchen echoed to her mirth. 'Went down in two shakes of a donkey's fetlock. Had to take another out of the freezer and it took an age to thaw, so it went in to cook a bit late, so . . . Not in any rush, are you? Go through and have a natter.'

Something in the way that Bridget said this sparked my suspicion. Notwithstanding disasters, she sounded chipper. Her broad grin pursued me out. Through the twilight of the living-room I discerned Patty on his knees at the hearth, feeding twelve-pounder hunks of larchwood to the wisps of flame fighting through the layers of ash in which the fire-basket was submerged, concomitantly launching smoke and fumes into asphyxiating spirals; only the draughts mitigated the toxic effect. At my appearance he abandoned his efforts.

'Hi-ya, Paul!' He made sturdy use of outmoded expressions, as if trapped uncomplainingly in a time-warp, as indeed he was. 'Sherry? Scotch? You've met Miss Peterson here? Angela, my dear, this is Paul Hunt, our esteemed neighbour and part-time courier: keeps the teashop in the village. Looks after the—'

'Angela knows all that, you silly old buffer.' Bridget, who had tailed me in, stood surveying us in triumph. 'Our schoolmarm,' she explained to me, 'is still on Easter holiday, so that's why she's here. We've been meaning to have her for weeks. When is it, Angela, you go back?'

'Tuesday.' The schoolteacher replied with composure, although I gained the impression that my arrival had tipped her slightly off balance. Privately deploring Bridget's social engineering, I gave my fellow-guest an amicable nod.

'We met yesterday. At the show.'

'I believe we did.'

'No bruises?'

'They haven't come out yet.'

Nursing a glass of sherry, she sat with her knees tidily arranged beneath a full, cream skirt topped by a red blouse with short sleeves. From where I stood, through the gloom, I could see the goose-pimples. I said rallyingly, 'Nice blaze, Patty, you've got coming along. Hang in there. I'll get my own drink. Logs lasting out?'

'I chop,' he returned lugubriously, prodding the embers, 'every morning of the week, from nine to eleven. Then Bridget brings me my hot chocolate. Couldn't do without my hot chocolate. Replaces the calories, y'know. Warms the body from within.'

'You only have it,' his wife said dispassionately, 'because you like the taste. Paul, I've got that little written message

for you: don't go off without it. What's that hound doing
on the sofa? He's meant to be in disgrace. Bad Reggie!
Carry on, you people, while I try and hurry things along.'
Giving me a vast and obvious wink, she returned to her
pots and pans. I eyed Angela's glass.

'Like a top-up?'

'I'm fine, thanks.'

I helped myself to whisky, adding some ginger with an
eye to survival. 'So, you've taken over from Miss Somerby?
How do you find the little terrors?'

'I just make my way to the classroom each morning and
there they are.'

Patty released a snort. 'Put yourself in line for that one,
Paul. You won't get past our Angela that easily.'

'I wasn't trying to,' I said mildly. 'I just wondered if they
needed a rod of iron. You hear such tales.'

'Angela's good with children. The parents all say so.'

I smiled across at her. 'You'll have to write a textbook
on the subject. These days, it should be a bestseller.'

She said nothing. I felt uncomfortably that I had put my
foot in it, without comprehending why. Absorbed in his
fire-raising, Patty remained heedless of the atmosphere. To
kick-start the dialogue in a new direction I said, 'Patty, I
wanted to ask you something. I'm getting noises.'

He glanced round with his eyes watering. 'What did you
say?'

'Noises, at night. I can't trace the source of them and
they're keeping me awake.'

Hoisting himself upright, Patty seized his whisky glass
and made for the chair which was recognized as his, at
some distance from the fireplace and in the very teeth of
the fiercest draught, the one that whiplashed from the
highly visible gap in the wall masonry at the back of the
room, overlooking the valley across which the east wind
threw itself at the house. He and Bridget were always

intending to have the fissure looked at. The structure, I suspected, was terminally unsafe, and fate would determine whether or not either or both of them were in occupation when it eventually collapsed about their ears. Seating himself like a High Court judge, our host regarded me broodingly through the fog.

'Creaks? Rattles? These old cottages, y'know—'

'Oh, I'm used to that kind of thing. This is something else. Hard to describe. Sort of a thumping, wailing sound. Weird.'

'Fox? Badger?'

'Do they make sounds like that? Anyway, it seems to come from inside.'

'Squirrels? They can get in under the eaves.'

'I've had squirrel trouble before. Nothing like this.'

Bridget reappeared at the doorway. 'Subsidence.'

'What?'

'Wall movement.' She pointed dramatically. 'We know all about that. Remind me, Patty, to telephone Goodman some time. We really must get something done.'

'In my case,' I said, 'I doubt if it's settlement. It's just not that kind of a noise.'

'The wind can beat through, you know, like nobody's business.'

'It happens on calm nights.'

'Any particular time?'

'Late evening.'

Bridget pursed her lips. 'Nothing to do with the TV, or radio?'

'Funny you should say that. Last night . . .'

I hesitated. The schoolteacher was observing me with a look of cool assessment, as though I were on my feet reciting from a desk in the third row. I decided to go on. 'I'd been watching the soccer. When the match was over I went upstairs to bed. An hour or so later, as I was dropping off to sleep, I heard this chanting . . .'

'*Chanting?*' Bridget echoed explosively.

'That's what it sounded like. When I went downstairs to investigate, there was this heavy vibration filling the room, and on top of that the damn TV had switched itself on again: it was showing a repeat of a Promenade concert from last year, some modern work for chorus and strings. How do you account for that?'

'I suppose somebody thought there was an audience for it.'

'I meant, how did the set come back on?'

'Had you switched it off?'

'I'm certain I did.'

'You were sleepy,' Patty said weightily, 'and you thought you'd turned it off but you hadn't.'

'I remember pressing the button.'

'It was Phoebe, then,' pronounced Bridget.

I looked at her blankly. 'Who's Phoebe?'

'Haven't you heard? Phoebe, the kitchenmaid from the Manor. Ill-used by the Squire at the turn of the century. According to legend, she put an end to herself in your cottage, where she lived at the time. Or it may be Myrtle's, next door. One of the two.' Bridget beamed around the room. 'Perhaps the poor girl's bobbed up again.'

'Pull the other one.'

'Patty will bear me out,' she protested. 'It's a documented case. If Phoebe is a tormented soul, she probably doesn't think much of your TV programmes, so she switches them on and off. That's my explanation. Meanwhile, Patty, the duck's ready to carve.'

Left to ourselves, the schoolteacher and I studied our drinks. She looked composed, self-sufficient, as though not in need of verbal exchanges. For some reason I was nettled by this. After a moment I said, 'How many are you teaching, at the moment?'

She remained silent. I was about to repeat the question when she looked up, and I realized that she had been giving it careful thought. 'Thirty-three, just now. The class size is thirty-five. Two off sick.'

I nodded politely. 'Any troublemakers?'

'Not really.'

'How does it compare with your previous school?'

'Similar.'

'What led you to switch?'

'Perhaps I thought I needed a change.' She sipped at her sherry. 'I like this area.'

'Living near the school?'

She changed position, as if bracing herself to accommodate the tiresome nosiness of a pupil. 'You know Tussock Street? Downhill from the church. I'm renting a cottage belonging to George Curtis, the garage-owner.'

'Hoping to buy, eventually?'

She shrugged. 'I haven't made any specific plans.'

A lead weight fell across the conversation, exterminating it. I added another splash of soda to my whisky. From the kitchen came sounds of expostulation as Patty did something to the duckling that offended Bridget's notion of what was seemly. The schoolteacher caught my eye. She didn't smile, but she seemed to be jolted into involuntary speech. 'Have you bought yours?'

'I'm sorry? Oh—yes. Got it cheap because it was dropping to bits.'

'So you had things done to it?'

'Not enough things, evidently.'

'The noises?'

I nodded. Suddenly I was bored with the topic of rural habitations. Appearing to sense this, Angela made a big effort. 'Were you in catering before?'

'Before I took over the Pantiles? No, I wasn't.'

She waited. I left it at that, and before she could prompt me—assuming that she had any intention of doing so, which seemed open to doubt—Bridget called us through to the dining recess to partake of white-hot vegetable soup. A sealed envelope stood against my plate, buckling gently in the vapour. 'For the Mystery Lady,' she informed me. 'Don't bury it in an inside pocket and forget about it. I want her to have it as soon as possible.'

'Tomorrow morning,' I promised.

'And see if you can snatch a word with her, Paul, while you're at it. We ought to find out her name, at least.'

'Bridget's on thorns,' Patty informed the table at large. 'Anonymity is the ultimate crime in these parts.'

'It's just a matter of trying to be friendly. The soup might taste a little burned. I forgot it for a moment and the cooker suddenly flared. We'll have to get it looked at, Patty. One of these days you're going to come in and find me running around the kitchen with my hair alight. Then you'll have to make your own hot chocolate. Angela, my dear, there's something I've been meaning to ask. According to the Rector . . .'

The meal passed, for me, less comfortably than usual. An ingredient was missing: the easy interchange of chaff between the Sheeneys and myself. It was, I had to acknowledge, no direct fault of Angela's. She could equally have blamed me for casting a blight across the table. The pair of us simply didn't hit it off. As soon as decently acceptable after pretending to drink Bridget's lethal coffee around the fire, now a mound of inert dust which Patty wisely ignored, I made my excuses. 'Gillian,' I explained, 'will be needing a break. She's been there since eight-thirty this morning.'

'That's right, Paul, you look after her.' Bridget came to the door to see me off. 'You and Angela must come again,' she confided in a whisper that carried to the bedrooms.

'The two of you get along so well. Same day next week?'

'I'll let you know, Bridget, if I may. Gillian may be having a day or two off, in which case—'

'You'll be tied to the shop. Wait and see, then. You've got the letter for Prior's Farm?'

'Delivery guaranteed,' I said, patting my breast pocket.

'*Should* you get to speak to her, ask whether she'd be willing to take on the Stationery Stall. I've nobody earmarked for that.'

My route back from Timbers took me across agricultural land by way of a pockmarked track barely wider than the Land-Rover's wheelbase. In place of the former hedgerows, triple-railed fencing enclosed it from the wheat-planted fields that fell away steeply on either side. Intent upon the relief of Gillian, who was too priceless an asset to risk offending, I throttled down hard and took the stretch at a gallop.

Some way ahead, a tractor attached to a cart stood at rest in an offside gateway. At the wheel sat a motionless figure, reading a newspaper. As I approached, I noticed him folding the newsprint in leisurely manner, putting it aside while making adjustments to his woolly hat, a tea-cosy affair in a vivid shade of orange which matched the stripes painted on my vehicle for purposes of maximum visibility. The tractor itself was bright yellow. Both of us could be seen for miles. At a point thirty yards from the gateway, I noticed faint shuddering movements in the region of his rear wheels.

My foot hovered above the brake pedal.

The tractor gave a lurch, halted again. My foot returned to the accelerator. At the same instant, another lurch snatched my attention, tossed me into two minds; I couldn't decide whether to pull up or take evasive action, and by the time I had weighed the options I was running out of space. Moreover, conditions were against me. This part of the track had recently played host to an assembly of prime Jersey cattle which had left in its wake a surface spread of liquidized clay with all the grip and stability of lubricating grease. With a sickening sense of disaster, I felt the wheels of the Land-Rover spin, then glide.

Helpless, I heard the explosive impact as the front near-side of the vehicle skated into the fence. The rails disintegrated to allow us through. With the wheel jumping uselessly in my grasp, I had a swift impression of endless green acres stretching ahead of and below me: then I was bucketing over furrows with other things rushing at me. A lower line of fencing, a belt of trees, the lip of a ravine.

From the top, it had seemed a long way down. The distance had been covered with amazing speed. The trees, I had time to observe, were of the substantial variety, shielding a watercourse that burrowed deep into the earth. With a feeling of utter hopelessness I pumped the footbrake.

At the same time I wrenched at the wheel. The leading tree slid off to the right. Then it came back at me. It was alongside, nosing the offside panels in a screech of timber and metal. Indulging in a final bounce, the Land-Rover planted its wheels like a spaniel digging its paws in, and came to rest in a low hissing.

Unclipping the seat-belt, I crawled across to the nearside door and tumbled out on to the ruts. My eardrums sang. Looking up, I saw a woolly-hatted figure at lane level, silhouetted against the skyline. It was brandishing both arms.

'You could've been killed,' gasped Gillian.

The possibility, I told her, had not escaped me. My immediate concern was how to dispose of her kindly-administered black coffee without harm to her feelings. So soon after Bridget's toxic offering, it was making me feel sick. 'In an ordinary saloon,' I said, upending the mixture furtively into an empty confectionery tin at the end of the counter and snapping the lid, 'I'd have been rather flatter than I am now, with my feet facing opposite ways.'

'Ooh, don't.'

'When I chose an off-road runabout, that wasn't quite the sort of deviation I had in mind.'

'Is there much dammidge?'

'A twisted door-arch and a snapped exhaust. George Curtis says I should get it back tomorrow.'

'Did he come out to give you a tow?'

'No. The tractor bloke hauled me up. I suppose he thought it was the least he could do.'

'I should think so, after making you swerve like that. Will you be taking him to court?'

Laughter escaped from me. 'It was pure accident. I over-reacted. As he said, he was just starting to nose out of the gateway and there was plenty of room for me to slip past if I hadn't panicked.'

'Still, he ought to be more careful. Who was it?'

'Kevin Somebody.'

'Kevin Riley.' Gillian nodded sternly. 'Works for Cyril Blake at Starks Farm. No more common sense than he was born with, that boy. All he thinks about is gadgets. Shouldn't never have charge of a tractor.'

'By his reckoning, I shouldn't be allowed behind a wheel either. Let's call it quits.'

Gillian's return to the kitchen to attend to her ginger snaps gave me the opportunity to dispose of the confectionery tin in the waste receptacle. Roger Ashby caught me in the act. 'What's that swishing sound, old boy—melted acid drops? Not blood, I trust. Hear you've just cheated extinction. A shade premature, weren't you? Moto-cross trials aren't till next month.'

'For God's sake,' I said, 'it only happened an hour ago. How did you come to hear already?'

He smiled fatly. 'Just called in at the garage for a fill-up. Spotted that battered hulk of yours in the workshop having its ribs hammered out, so naturally I made inquiries. Glad to see you're intact.' He studied me more closely. 'Or do I detect a certain tautness of the upper lip?'

'It was that mention of ribs. Mine are complaining a bit. Otherwise I'm fine, except that I've got indigestion. I'm off home soon to take a couple of Rennies, a painkiller, a sleeping draught and a tranquillizer: by this time tomorrow I'll be either back to normal or dead.'

Feeling in a pocket, he produced a phial. 'Try one of these.'

'What are they?'

'Knock-out drops. Sal has them on prescription. She has problems sleeping at times.'

'Thanks, but I won't deprive her. Why are you studying those biscuits?'

He selected two tins. 'Sal's at home to the Ladies' Poetry Circle tomorrow afternoon, so she asked me to lay in stocks. I'll be out for the day.' Palms pressed together, he made a pantomime of giving thanks to Heaven. 'It's on occasions like this I'm grateful for having a respectable occupation that takes me away from the house. I've nothing against verse, as long as I don't have to read or hear it.'

'What's respectable about property speculation?'

'You tell me, old boy. On the other hand, what's praiseworthy about poverty?'

'If you've profits to chuck around,' I suggested, 'you could do worse than consider another branch of the arts.'

'What might that be?'

I nodded towards the tea-room. 'On display through there, if you haven't already noticed, are four pictures of local landmarks painted by a local artist, going for a song. How about it? Sally might fancy one for the living-room.'

Ashby wrinkled his nose. 'We did take a look at 'em, last

time we were here. Good stuff, of its type. Not quite our style, though. A bit . . . representational for my taste.' He subjected me to a leer. 'Seeing you're struck on her work, why don't you have one of 'em yourself?'

'I did buy the first one she brought in. I'd prefer the next purchaser to be someone else.'

'I get you. Let me think about it. Forty quid's forty quid, these hard times.'

'Climb off it, Roger. In case you've forgotten, you once bragged to me that with Sally's income from her inheritance you need never lift a finger again. Either you were shooting a line—'

'I wasn't,' he said smugly, taking no offence, as I had known he wouldn't.

'Well, then. How about a smidgeon of support for a deserving case?'

'I said, I'll think about it. How are you getting home this evening, by the way?'

'George Curtis has lent me a Fiesta.'

'He'll stick the price on the repair bill, you'll see. Nothing's for nothing.'

'You should know,' I said rudely.

'When you're blessed with a business brain,' he said equably, 'it seems only sensible to make use of it. 'Bye now, Paul. Watch out for steamrollers.'

He was through the door before I could throw anything.

CHAPTER 4

The spectacle of Myrtle Jones hovering near my front gate was not beneficial to my spirits. ''Evening, Myrtle,' I said pointedly. 'If it's a cup of sugar you're after—'

'I don't want to borrow anything, Paul. It's just that we

heard about your close shave this afternoon. We're so sorry, Don and I. If there's anything—'

'No harm done. My own fault for being careless.'

'I'm sure you were nothing of the kind. That stretch of lane can be very dicey. Besides, that farm hand—'

'He was most helpful afterwards. Hauled me out, gave me a tow into the village. No complaints.'

Myrtle sniffed. 'In your position,' she declared, shielding her eyes to examine me as if scanning for hairline fractures, 'I'd have kicked up a dust, I can tell you. Some of these agricultural drivers think they own the roads, as well as the fields.'

'Well, they were here before I was. You'll have to excuse me, Myrtle, I'm expecting a phone call from the garage. Thanks for dropping round.'

'Well, we thought it was only neighbourly. Oh Paul, did you remember—'

'Sent the order form off this morning.'

'Oh good. Don had another look this morning and he says the level is up quite a bit more.'

'Courage, Myrtle. The Refuse Department's Seventh Cavalry should be riding over the horizon within days.'

Leaving her blank-faced by the gatepost, I escaped to my kitchen, which doubled as the cottage's entrance hall. Here I stood irresolute for some moments, trying to decide whether I wanted a cooked meal. Regardless of the lunchtime fiasco, I had no appetite. What I really yearned for, I discovered, was a horizontal posture between warm sheets. Munching a couple of dry biscuits, I switched on the TV to capture the tail-end of the newscast, listened to—and forgot immediately—the weather forecast, flicked the screen back to a vacancy which matched that of Myrtle's countenance, and went upstairs. Drawing the curtains, I undressed and fell into bed. For a while I lay wakeful, re-examining the events of the day.

*

Eleven-forty.

As I blinked at them, the illuminated numerals of the bedside digital clock/radio jumped to eleven-forty-four. The thing had an erratic tendency. In a minute or two, they would leap back to eleven-forty-two, and then forward to the three-quarters. By and large, however, they were reasonably accurate. If they told me it was nearing midnight, I believed them.

It was late, I thought, clambering blearily out of bed, for someone to be phoning. Despite what I had told Myrtle, I was expecting no calls. Was it a bell I could hear? The sound that came from below was low and muffled, more human than mechanical. The chill I felt as I groped for the bedroom door handle was not entirely due to the room temperature.

The bottom of the staircase was separated from the living-room by another door. Taking breath before opening it, I felt a spasm of pain from a lower rib, and concluded that now was not the time for heroics. If an intruder confronted me, I should offer him a drink and one of the better ornaments and send him on his way. Then I could get back to sleep. The door drifted wide, and I was greeted by a voice.

'We need to talk. Things can't be left as they are. It's fair to no one.'

Whom did I know with a Californian accent? Abruptly it dawned upon me that the TV screen was alive once more. A middle-aged man with a thatch of silver hair was addressing a young woman inside a cathedral, or possibly a six-bedroom apartment viewed through the wrong end of a telescope. Grabbing up the remote control device from its perch on a chair-arm, I sent the two of them packing, restoring silence and darkness to the room. I stood for a moment, listening. Then I went through to the kitchen.

The strip lighting showed me only normality. Outer door

fastened; nothing out of place. Returning warily to the living-room, I switched on more lights.

'Anybody around?'

The absurdity of the query hit me forcibly, but I felt I had to ask. Apart from myself, the room was manifestly unoccupied. I tested the security catches on the windows. All of them were clamped tight.

As I stood pondering, my feet began to vibrate.

Something heavy seemed to be throwing itself around beneath the floorboards, preparatory to bursting through the carpet. The vibration became a shudder, increasing steadily in intensity. Nervously I backed off to the kitchen doorway, eyeing the furniture. It seemed likely at any minute to separate and make for the walls, leaving space at the centre for . . . what?

My imagination stampeded. Behind the shuddering, other sounds were distinguishable. Squeaks and sighs; cracking noises, like floorboards being forced up. And everything was gaining in volume. The room seemed to have become a studio for sound effects, tested to destruction. Stepping back into the kitchen, I slammed the connecting door, unlatched the outer one and escaped into the garden.

There was no moon, no starlight. I went back for the flashlight I kept in a kitchen drawer. The battery was almost extinct. Taking it outside, I aimed the feeble glow at the base of the exterior wall, following it along.

The brickwork seemed intact. Rounding the corner, I investigated the front of the cottage beneath the main window. Both airbricks were undamaged. There was no sign anywhere of an entry point.

The torchlight expired. Total blackness enfolded me. The lane, four yards away on the other side of the gate, was invisible. No movements of any kind. But still I could plainly hear the internal throbbing.

I forced myself back to the kitchen.

Although I didn't want it, I made coffee. I needed time to reflect. In the next room, the pounding and shuddering went on, causing the connecting door to rattle. Sipping desperately at the coffee, I hit out at the lower panel of the door with my slippered foot, as if this would somehow restore silence. What it did was to damage my big toe. While I was nursing it, cursing aloud, I considered phoning the Sheeneys. There were several arguments against this. One was that it would involve crossing the animated living-room floor to get to the handset by the window. That achieved, what should I say? *I'm having a nightmare. Would you mind coming along to poke me out of it?* Bridget and Patty were a lively pair but they were, after all, octogenarians. There must be a limit to the demands of friendship.

The urge remained to make contact with somebody. Even the Joneses came into my reckoning, but my reluctance in their case was still greater. The bond stemming from a preoccupation with cesspool drainage fell short of total rapport. Who else was there? Prior's Farm was the next habitation along. If the Dark Lady shunned visitors by day, she was unlikely to welcome a midnight call for assistance; and besides, she was not on the telephone. Nobody else of my acquaintance was closer than a couple of miles. By the time they arrived . . .

At this point in my cogitation, the hubbub cut out.

It was as though a soundproof screen had been dropped suddenly into place. Fearful of relaunching the disturbance, I delayed opening the living-room door; I stood holding my breath and the door handle, listening intently, waiting for everything to come back at me. Finally, feeling an idiot, I pressed down the lever and kicked the door wide open. Silence and stillness greeted me.

A second tour of the room revealed nothing. Each item of furniture stood on its appointed spot. Every book remained stiffly in line on its shelf. The newspapers lay on the sofa where I had left them. All the cushions were in place. And, contrary to what I had half-expected, the carpet looked as flat and placid as when it was first laid.

I was half way through breakfast when the telephone shrilled. Spitting out bacon rind, I covered the plate and went through to answer. The voice was unfamiliar.

'Mr Paul Hunt, is that?'

I said cautiously that it was. He sounded ominously like a dissatisfied customer or trade supplier. 'Blake here,' he informed me. 'Starks Farm.'

'Good morning, Mr Blake.' I put my intonation into neutral. 'Not met, have we? Something I can do for you?'

'Sorry if it's a mite early for you.' The faint contempt of the land worker for the indolent townsman was inherent in the remark. 'I just wanted . . . I thought I should inquire how you were, following your little contretemps yesterday with one of my blokes. I'm told you weren't hurt—is that right?'

'Happily I was well strapped in and the Land-Rover stayed upright. Apart from a bruised rib, I'm fine. Good of you to ask.'

'I've had a word with Riley. He tells me that in his opinion he left adequate space for you to get through. There should have been no—'

'I'm not arguing.'

'You're not?' The farmer's tone underwent subtle alteration. 'You don't dispute that version of the incident, then?'

'Not a bit. It all happened rather fast.'

'Well, they do, of course, these . . . miscalculations. Glad it was no worse. Much damage to the vehicle?'

'Fairly minor.'

'That's good. Decent of you to take it this way, Mr Hunt.' The sweat of relief emanated almost palpably from the receiver. 'Ever look in at the Stag? Be glad to buy you a drink, next time you're there.'

'Look forward to it.'

'In the meantime,' he said guardedly, 'if there's anything at all I can do to help out . . . How about transport?'

'No problem. I've the loan of a car from George Curtis.'

'Fine. Well, nice talking to you, Mr Hunt. I'll leave you to—'

'There is something, though, you might be able to advise me on.'

'Uh-huh?'

'As a farming man,' I said diffidently, 'you'd know more about wild creatures than I do. Rodents, for example. Just how much disturbance can they create?'

He hooted briefly. 'Given the right circumstances—the wrong ones, that is—there's virtually no limit. Why do you ask?'

'I've been having some trouble at nights, here in the cottage.' I gave him an edited version of events. 'Could something like that possibly be down to rats or mice, operating in numbers?'

'There's not much I'd put past the little blighters,' said Blake after a pause. 'That phrase, *Quiet as a mouse*—it's balderdash, you know. I certainly wouldn't rule it out. Tried putting poison down?'

'Not yet.'

'I'd give it a bash. What was that you said, about the TV? Turns itself on and off?'

'On, anyhow. It did occur to me that some pest might have nibbled partly through the wiring somewhere, making a loose connection. That feasible?'

'I'd have thought, in that case, you'd get dodgy reception the whole time: not come and go.' There was another brief silence. 'When you switch the set off at night, do you do it from the socket?'

'As a rule, I douse it with the remote control and leave it at that till morning.'

'Where do you keep the control?'

'Side of my chair.'

'If a rat or mouse,' he said slowly, 'were at large in the room, it could quite easily scuttle across it?'

'Ah. I see what you mean.'

'It could tread on one of the buttons,' he enlarged help-fully, 'and so reactivate the set. Just a thought.'

'You may well have something. They're a bit hair-trigger, in fact. Takes very little to press them down.'

'Only a theory,' Blake said modestly. 'If you like, though, I could have a word with Riley about it. He's by way of being something of a technician. Between us, we could pick his brains over a pint. Don't forget, then. One night this week, maybe, at the Stag?'

'I hope so. Thanks for calling, Mr Blake. Tell Kevin he's not to worry. I appreciated the tow.'

The bacon was cold and stiff when I got back to it. Throwing the dishes into the sink, I abandoned them for later and drove the Fiesta circumspectly the three miles into the village. Gillian had opened up and was at work upon the morning batch of scones.

'Feeling more lively, Mr Hunt?'

'No. But less deadly. That looks a bigger mix than usual. Are we expecting a rush?'

'Bit of a nip in the air this morning,' she explained earn-estly. 'They'll all be clamouring for hot scones with their coffees, you mark my words.'

'I hope you're right. Look, Gill, I'm not going to leave you in the lurch again today. But I'll be out at lunch-time for half an hour, no longer. OK by you?'

'Take as long as you want, Mr Hunt,' she said generously. 'I'll be here. Oh—Mrs Guttridge was in again after you left last night . . .'

'What does she want now?'

'Said to tell you her nephew's in the motor trade and if you need any repair jobs doing she can get you a discount.'

'Plus a rake-off for herself. I just hope I've still got her nose for business at the age of ninety-two.'

Inquiries after my state of health dominated the morning. Bridget telephoned to bay her and Patty's relief at my survival, urging me to abandon four-wheel drive and invest in a bicycle. 'Keeps you fit, and you'll save on petrol. Good for dodging through gaps, as well. Can't have you crocking yourself, my dear. All the village maidens will be inconsolable.'

'They seem to be controlling their anxiety at the moment.'

'Don't you believe it. Angela rang me last evening. She was most concerned.'

'The schoolteacher?'

'Your fellow-guest yesterday,' she bellowed. 'She'd heard you'd been half-killed.'

'Could there have been an element of wishful thinking? Let's face it, Bridget, I wasn't the greatest hit with her, was I?'

'Phwat in the world are you talking about? Not a hit? I was just saying to Patty—'

'If Angela was so upset about me, she only had to lift the phone.'

'Didn't want to disturb you. Thought you might be resting.'

'She was right there. Anyway, I'm back in shape this morning. I'll be leaving soon for Prior's Farm.'

'If you see the lady, ask her—'

'Calm down, Bridget. I shan't, and she won't, and you haven't. I'm only making the trip because you and Lionel

Felrose have asked me to, and because I might even pick up a spot of business myself. If half of what people say is true, she must need reprovisioning by now. Why shouldn't I cash in?'

'Why ever not, my dear? Best of luck. Mind how you drive.'

Although Gillian was right and it had turned colder, the persistent moistness of recent days had vanished from the atmosphere, allowing the lane surfaces to dry out. It felt odd, driving a conventional hatchback again. Midway along Parsons Lane I passed Myrtle, walking Pudge their labrador; I waved through the window and got another blank look in response. To Myrtle I was simply a car, threatening her space. A pity, I thought ungenerously, that I couldn't remain as anonymous to her at other times, in particular when she was uptight about sewage.

The concreted track which ran from the lane down one side of a shallow valley to Prior's Farm had collapsed over the neglected years into a replication of the moon's surface, presenting formidable obstacles to a civilized approach. I missed the Land-Rover. Bouncing gamely from fissure to outcrop, the Fiesta took me around the ultimate bend where a barn with a sagging roof stood guard at a gateway that gave access to a gravelled yard, littered with junk ranging from a rusted scythe to a heap of treadless tractor tyres to a hay cart flat on its axles. To one side stood the farmhouse, stone-built to first-floor level where it became tile-hung, and roofed with slate to which sepia-green fungus had attached itself in quantity. Any paint remaining on the doors and window-frames had largely parted company with the timber to hang in coiled strips, waiting to drop off. An immense and ramshackle chimneystack at one end of the roof looked equally insecure: one gust, it seemed, would have pitched it through the slating into the loft. Surveying the hulk through the windscreen of the car as I applied the handbrake, I wondered just what kind of rustic solitude the mystery tenant had been seeking, and whether she had found it. She was either sturdily independent or somebody with a problem. In either case, Bridget's hopeful invitation to a bring-and-buy sale looked a non-starter, although Lionel Felrose's plea for antiques might, I thought, stand a marginally better chance.

A third of the way up from the base of the tongued-and-grooved door facing the yard, there was a letter flap. Before making use of it, I gave the woodwork a rap with my knuckles, waited a moment, repeated the action with more vigour, waited again, looked around vainly for a bell-push or knocker, eyed the curtained window alongside the door, then pushed the letters through and returned to the car. I could now truthfully inform Bridget that I had made efforts to claim attention. About to ignite the engine, I remembered what the Rector had said about a Fiat. Emerging once more, I tramped round to the back of the farmhouse.

There it stood, a deep-blue minicar with its skirts caked with mud. I tried the doors: they were locked, as the Rector's wife Polly had reported. The impression given off by the car was that it had been there, unused, since its owner's arrival. The front offside tyre was almost flat. With a shrug I returned to the Fiesta. I had the door open and was stooping to get inside when a voice hit me between the shoulder-blades.

'Paul!'

Twisting about, I saw that the boarded door now stood open. A figure was emerging. There was a smile on its face. The rest of its body was clad in sweater and jeans, featureless enough to rob it of identity; but there was no mistaking the voice. 'Well, well,' it added, as she approached, 'I thought I wasn't mistaken. Fancy seeing you here, of all people. How are you, darling, and how did you track me down?'

CHAPTER 5

Five minutes after my return to the Pantiles, Lionel Felrose skipped across.

'That guff of mine,' he said anxiously. 'I was wondering—'

'It's been delivered,' I assured him.

'Wonderful! I knew I could count on you, Paul. You have a trustworthy air. The face of a . . .' He paused to peer at me. 'In point of fact, dear boy, you're looking a teeny bit green around the gills at the moment. Delayed shock, perhaps?'

'What do you mean?'

'Your motoring misadventure.' The sharpness of my answer took him aback. 'Only yesterday, wasn't it? You might have *ruptured* something. Have you been for a check-up?'

'I'm perfectly all right.'

'You honestly don't look it.' His scrutiny intensified.

'Lionel,' I said through gritted teeth, 'there's nothing wrong with me or my vitals. Your literature has gone to . . . to Prior's Farm: now you'll just have to wait and see if there's a response. There's nothing more I can do.'

'Naturally, I didn't expect . . .' He stood fidgeting. 'You didn't by any chance make personal contact with the incumbent?'

'I was pushed for time. Had to get back here to relieve Gillian.'

'Yes, of *course*.' He regarded me covertly from under his lashes. 'I still think, you know, you're looking quite peaky. Sleeping all right? Sometimes, after a shock to the nervous system . . .'

'My nervous system will be fine, thank you, once left to its own devices.'

His yellowed front teeth displayed themselves to me. 'Message received,' he said playfully, 'and understood. Look after yourself, Paul. Don't ignore any tiny signals: that's all I'd advise. They can increase, you know, and multiply. You've got a customer, I'd better get along. 'Afternoon, Mrs Guttridge. Saucier than ever in your spring bonnet.'

'Same as me autumn one,' she chortled, fingering the cloche abomination that adhered to her skull through the seasons. 'Got them fancies for us, Mr Hunt? Them what you promised?'

I looked at her vacantly. Lionel had taken his departure, leaving the two of us eyeball to eyeball across the counter: try as I might to make sense of what she had just said, I couldn't. Luckily the kitchen door flung itself back at this moment to disgorge the hunched figure of Gillian supporting a tray of pastries. 'These what you was after, Mrs G? Fresh made this morning. Lots of cream, like you said. Your grandson, is it, and his friend from school? Plus his little sister? Reckon you'll be needing all of them.' Packing the cakes into Mrs Guttridge's bag, Gillian turned her face to me. 'What we charging for the eclairs, Mr Hunt?'

'I don't know. What do you think?'

The eyes of both of them widened. Mrs Guttridge tittered. 'Not here along of us, he ain't. Off in a world of his own. Have 'em for free, like, shall I?'

'Sort it out between you,' I said. 'I'll be in the kitchen, Gill, if I'm wanted.'

A few minutes later she followed me in. I summoned a smile to aim at her. 'Not too hectic while I was gone?'

'No. Fairly quiet, reely.'

'Sorry I was a bit longer than I said I'd be.'

'That's OK.' Removing another tray from the range oven, she bore it over to a corner worktop and inspected its contents critically before turning the same look upon me, as if comparing textures. 'You all right, Mr Hunt?'

'Don't I look it?'

'You don't sound it. Sure you wasn't hurt yesterday?'

'People keep asking me that. If I had been, I'd have fallen apart by now. What I need is a good night's sleep.'

'Can't do without your kip,' Gillian said wisely. 'You don't look yourself, I must say. Reely washed out. Why don't you stop on in here for a bit, have a quick forty winks? I can look after the shop.'

'I keep imposing on you.'

'What I'm here for,' she said in motherly fashion. 'You get your feet up, Mr Hunt, and see if you can nod off. There's brandy in the cupboard, if you fancy a drop.'

It seemed like good advice. With the kitchen to myself, I poured a tot of cognac and sat nursing a mouthful while staring at the quarry-tiled floor. I had much to think about.

Elaine's face was thinner and paler than I remembered, but when she took off her beret and let her hair tumble, the strands were of the same shimmering red-gold that had since stalked me sporadically in my dreams . . . or nightmares. Perched on the rim of the central table inside the unwelcoming scullery of the farmhouse, she kept the smile on her lips while appraising me with the fathomless green eyes that awakened more echoes. 'Who'd have thought it?' she breathed. 'Can it possibly be coincidence? Or did you follow me here?'

'Me? Follow *you*?'

She gave me an exaggerated wince. 'No need to say it like that.'

'I'll say it how I please.'

'You don't sound too friendly, Paul Pot. Has it come as such a shock to you, me being here?'

'Let's just say, I was quite happy up to five minutes ago. Now I'm less happy.'

'That's frank, at all events.' She motioned me into a tall-backed wooden chair. 'But then you always were one for speaking your mind, as I recall. That's probably why you were regarded as promising managerial substance. Shame it had to end in the way it—'

'Talking of coincidence,' I interrupted, 'I might ask you the same question. Was it a chance in a thousand . . . or did you choose to anchor yourself here because you knew I was a near neighbour?'

She raised her eyebrows. 'Don't flatter yourself, Paul Pot. We may have had some good times, but I was never that stuck on you. The reasons for my being here . . . Well, that'll keep. What do you think of my abode?'

I glanced around. 'Want me to speak my mind again?'

'Not necessary,' she said carelessly. 'I'm only renting, you know. Six months' lease. By the end of that time I'm hoping things will have sorted themselves out.'

'Things?'

'Those reasons I mentioned. So, Paul. What are you getting up to? Not animal husbandry? Don't tell me. Somehow I don't see you in boots and corduroys, milking cows at four a.m.'

'I keep a teashop.'

'Never! Does it turn a profit? All cakestands and copper kettles, type of thing? My! And a general store? That must keep you busy. Would you have time to do me a favour?'

'I think you've had all the favours I can spare, Elaine.'

'You'd be doing yourself one, too, in this case. The thing is, I'm running short of supplies. I don't get out, you see, and although I brought a fair bit with me it's starting to dwindle at a rather alarming rate. Maybe you could help

stock me up again. Cash deal,' she added sweetly. 'You like
your financial transactions all above board, I know.'

I nodded my head at the window. 'That your Fiat round
the back?'

'Yes.'

'What's stopping you from going out, then?'

'Long story,' she said coolly. 'What it boils down to is,
at the moment I daren't. I'm reliant on others. So, if I were
to make you out a list, Paul Pot . . .'

'Must you keep calling me that?'

'It was my pet name for you. My Pot name.'

'When was I ever your pet?'

'My! We are grumpy.'

'Plaything. That I'll grant.'

'Let me fix you a drink. Something hot, or with ice?'

'I've already had the cold dowse, thank you. To be
brutally honest, Elaine, this hardly seems like a reunion
worth celebrating.'

She drifted languidly to the sink to run water into a kettle.
'I'm making instant coffee for myself. If the aroma gets to
you . . . let me know.' Plugging in the kettle, she switched
on and stood watching it. Without turning her head she
said, 'After three years, I'd have thought we could converse
like rational adults. Tell me about yourself, Paul. Country
living, Ye Olde Copper Kettle—everything. Does the lifestyle suit you?'

'If it didn't, I wouldn't be here.'

'I fancy not. Get along well, do you, with everyone?'

'By and large, they're a good crowd. Several cuts above
their urban counterparts.'

'Ouch! So you've no thought of leaving?'

'I've settled in.'

'How lovely. A Promised Land of your very own. You'd
be sorry to have to give it up.'

'Why should—' I stopped. 'You're leading up to something, Elaine. What is it?'

'Me? Nothing.' Drowning the coffee powder, she stirred it to a froth before bringing the cup back to the table. 'Swilling too much of this garbage,' she remarked, sipping with a shudder. 'Not a lot else to do, quite honestly. The thrills of a portable TV and a transistor don't take long to fade, I can tell you. Then of course there's eating, sleeping, taking a bath . . . You should see the toilet facilities, Paul. Early nineteenth-century, if that. The farmer who was here before—'

'Just why are you having to live like a fugitive, Elaine? Something you're afraid of?'

'Somebody.' She employed a teaspoon to remove something from the surface of her drink.

'A debt collector?'

'Don't be horrid. I don't owe anybody anything. I'm having to . . . lie low for a bit, that's all. There was a small misunderstanding.'

'Always a dab hand at misunderstandings, weren't you, Elaine? Other people's, that is. Not your own. You've always known exactly what you were doing.'

The green eyes glittered at me. 'Isn't that how one's meant to behave? Someone has to stay alert.'

'That certainly seems to apply to you, currently,' I said, observing her stiffen as a bird flew lightly against the window. 'You're here for six months, you said. What happens after that?'

She shrugged. 'Can't say, for sure.'

'To repeat my earlier question: what did make you choose this particular neck of the woods?'

'What made you choose it?'

'An old acquaintance who'd moved here notified me that the teashop was available.'

'Much the same in my case. This ruin was rented very

discreetly on my behalf, as a return for ... services
rendered. For the first week or so it was Heaven to be out
of circulation. Now, I'm so bored I could scream.'

'You'll be moving on, then, as soon as you feel you can?'

'That would please you, would it, Paul?'

'I'm not going to pretend I find your proximity
appealing.'

'You've grown pompous, my sweet, since last we spoke.
I may have to disappoint you. Much as I loathe it here,
that's not to say it doesn't serve its purpose. Well off the
beaten track, you've got to admit. Not costing me a penny.
If anybody did come snooping, they'd have a job finding
me. There's a dozen places upstairs I could melt into and
nobody the wiser. I could do a lot worse.'

'Each to his taste.'

'Besides, summer's coming, isn't it? The weather can
make a big difference. I might get to quite like it.'

I sat contemplating her.

She aimed a dreamy smile into her cup. 'One can't keep
everlastingly scuttling from point to point, can one? Sooner
or later, it's advisable to settle.'

'I don't see you as a country dweller, Elaine.'

'I never saw you as one. Life's chock full of surprises,
don't you think? Pass me that ballpoint, there's a love: I'll
be making a start on that list. You supply the basics, I
presume, like bread, cigarettes and so forth?'

'I've no wish to get involved with you, Elaine, ever
again.'

'But you've your business reputation to protect,' she murmured, commencing to scrawl. 'You wouldn't want to get
known round here as ... unreliable.'

I said softly, 'Just what do you mean by that?'

The green-eyed gaze flickered in my direction. 'You said
yourself, Paul Pot, you've built up a good relationship with
the folk in these parts. Carved a niche for yourself. You'd

hardly want to spoil the situation. That's all I meant.'

'The only reason—'

'So, if I give you the list, it won't take you any time to bundle everything together and fetch it along. No rush. Tomorrow morning will be fine. I'll have the coffee brewing. Your mouth might be drier by then.'

At eleven that night, when the noise from downstairs became insufferable, I stepped into my daytime shoes, wrapped myself in a sheepskin jacket and opened the bedroom door with a slam against the wall, as if that in itself might achieve something. It didn't. As I descended the stairs the racket got louder. By the time I reached the living-room it was hurting my eardrums.

The entire room was a ferment of sound. The floorboards shook. Crossing to the window, I grabbed the phone and carried it out to the kitchen, where the vibration was less deafening. Shutting the internal door, I stabbed out a number.

'That you, Don?'

'Don Jones speaking.' The voice of Myrtle's husband never failed to enrage me. Its compound of obsequiousness and self-satisfaction seemed to have been formulated to chew at my nerve-ends. At this moment, however, I was very nearly glad to hear it.

'Did I get you out of bed?'

'That's Paul, is it? No, I just got back with Pudge. Late walkies. What's up, chum?'

'You'll think this is bloody ridiculous,' I said carefully, 'but I'm having a spot of bother and I was wondering . . . I suppose you wouldn't feel like stepping round?'

'What sort of—'

'You'll see when you get here.'

'Give us a couple of minutes.'

For all my dislike of the man, I had to allow that he was

not disobliging. On the contrary, he was almost too ready
to leap to attention, rather as if balancing some personal
ledger of commitment: each kindly act entered on the credit
side, ultimately to be totted up prior to a courteous demand
for payment, with undertones of faint menace. Waiting for
him at the kitchen door, I told myself not to let prejudice
run away with me. There was nothing he could do about
his manner. Mine probably grated on him, too. When he
heard the noise . . .

At this point in my thoughts, the hubbub died.

As abruptly as before, the cottage was marooned in stillness. The sole intrusion was the click of heels along the
cement path leading to the kitchen. A flashlamp shone into
my face. My neighbour was breathing a little hard. 'Come
as fast as I could. Thought you might have somebody along
of you. Threatening you, like.' He rotated the flashlamp
beam, unnecessarily in my opinion since I had lights
switched on everywhere. 'Have a break-in, did you?'

'Nothing like that.' I brandished an arm in despair. 'It
was a noise I wanted you to hear. Only it's stopped.'

'Noise? Stopped?' His puffy face turned in all directions.

I indicated the living-room. 'Through there. Pandemonium. Not the first time it's happened. Tonight was the
worst, though.'

'Then it finished?'

'Just a moment before you arrived.'

He peered at me. 'Not uncommon, y'know, hearing
things in these old places. Get a bit of movement, settlement, stressed joists . . .'

'I've taken all that into account. This is different.' I
thumped the wall in frustration. 'What can I say? It was
all happening—then suddenly it wasn't. Sorry to drag you
here on a fool's errand.'

'No sweat, pal. While I'm here, may as well take a look
around. What kind of noise, did you say?'

I did my best to describe it. He sucked in his cheeks. 'Could be a wire shorting. Arc-ing. Play merry hell, that can, with your sound systems.' Nudging past me, he opened the door into the living-room, gave it an inquisitive inspection. 'What you got laid on?'

'Only the TV. That did come on by itself a couple of times, but since then I've been switching off at the socket before going to bed, and that seems to have done the trick.'

Jones fell slowly to his knees, as if about to pray. He prodded at the pile of the carpet. 'Come up from the floor, you said?'

'That's how it seemed. Thumping and wailing sounds, as if . . .' I ransacked my brain for an analogy. Without waiting for further enlightenment Jones moved sideways to the skirting-board.

'Let's have it up.'

'The carpet? I don't know that I—'

Producing a Swiss Army knife, he selected a blade and sank it into the join. Lifting a two-yard stretch, he furled it back. 'Boards look healthy enough.' Having tapped them, he inserted the point of the blade and gouged out a splinter. 'No rot there. Ventilation can't be a problem.'

'Even if it were, could it possibly lead to all that?'

'Depend, wouldn't it? You could get a build-up of compressed air, like, that comes out in the odd burst. Or it might have some knock-on effect on the wiring. If the insulation's breaking down—'

'It was supposed to have been re-done before I moved in.' I pondered the exposed boards. 'How about the joists underneath?'

'I'll go fetch me tools. Won't take us a moment.'

'I think I'd sooner leave anything like that until daylight.' By now I just wanted to be rid of him. 'Very grateful to you, Don, for coming round. Give Myrtle my apologies for bringing you out.'

'What neighbours are for, isn't it?' He rose, dusting the knees of his trousers. 'Any more trouble, me old mate, you give us a shout. It's what we're here for. If we was in trouble, we'd want to feel we could call on you. It's a two-way—'

'Well, you know your help is appreciated. Care for a drink before you go back?'

'I'll skip it, if it's all the same to you. Myrtle's got this thing about alcoholic breath in bed,' he informed me, to my relief. I saw him to the gate. 'Have them boards up tomorrow, if I was you,' was his parting advice. I said I would certainly think about it, and returned to the kitchen.

From there back into the living-room was a short step for a man but a giant stride for a coward. Having accomplished it, I hastily kicked the carpet back into place before darting for the stairs, escaping to bed. I lay tensely, waiting for it all to start up again. The rest of the night passed without disturbance, but sleep was not on the agenda.

CHAPTER 6

'Ever so pale you're looking, Mr Hunt. Getting a comeback, are you?'

'Just a restless night. A comeback from what?'

'The accident,' Gillian said on a note of expostulation. 'Could've done somethink to yourself, couldn't you? I reckon you should go and see the doctor.'

'Apart from red-hot coals where my eyes ought to be, I feel a hundred per cent.'

'Well, you don't look it, that's all I can say. Here, listen, I was reading one of them medical books—'

'Scones done, Gillian?'

'Half an hour ago,' she said reproachfully. 'And the rock

cakes. And I've scrubbed all the tables. You don't have to worry yourself about anything, Mr Hunt, reely you don't.'

'Those days off you're due for,' I muttered, smitten with remorse, 'remind me about them, will you? I take you too much for granted, young lady.'

'No you don't.'

'Wait till you hear what I'm about to say. I'm going to have to abandon you again this morning . . . just for an hour. I've a delivery to make. Can you cope?'

''Course I can. You go right ahead, Mr Hunt. What's this?'

'It's a list of the stuff I'll be needing. If you can take care of the food, I'll concentrate on the other things.'

She frowned at the paper. 'Who's it for?'

'Prior's Farm.'

Instantly she was agog. 'Got an order from her, did you? Seen her, have you? What's she like? What's she called? Does she—'

'We only spoke briefly. She needs supplies and she can't get out.'

'Disabled, like, is she? They was saying, along at the supermarket, they reckoned she must have somethink wrong with her. Never showing her face. Was she—'

'If she's not in poor health now, she soon will be if we don't get a move on. Jump to it, Gill, there's a love. I'm slipping along to Bradley's for the magazines she wants. Shove everything into a cardboard box and I'll pick it up on my way back.'

'I'll have it all ready,' she said compliantly.

When I got back with the magazines and cigarettes, two packed boxes awaited me. I carried them out to the Land-Rover, which I had reclaimed from the garage that morning and which was now parked in its customary spot twenty yards from the Pantiles, where the Main Street broadened to provide an unofficial lay-by. Strictly speaking, it was not for parking, but the local constable and I had a working arrangement of mutual tolerance. Loading up, I thought with contrition of Gillian and the burden I was placing upon her thin though willing shoulders. Time off she was entitled to, and time off she would have. As soon as things settled back to normal.

Yesterday I had passed Myrtle with Pudge; today, at the identical spot, I had to pull over to make way for a motor-scooter approaching at a brisk pace. Its rider was unmistakable. On her photographic rounds, Sandra Millett habitually encased herself in such quantities of leather and fibres and tempered steel that it was a marvel she avoided spontaneous combustion as she went along. She acknowledged me with a wave of a bulbous arm. I gave her a honk. On the heels of my penitence towards Gillian came a sense of shame at my recent self-absorption. Some people had real troubles to contend with.

From outside, Prior's Farm looked no livelier. The windows were still blanked out. The sole visible difference was provided by fresh tyre tracks in the gravel, which I thought had probably been made by the Fiesta I was driving the previous day. Halting the Land-Rover in the middle of them, I opened up the rear and took out the boxes, handling them with no great ceremony in case she was observing me from somewhere. I didn't want her to get the idea that I was jumping to her bidding, even if that was what it amounted to. Leaving one box on the gravel, I carried the other to the scullery door and gave it a hammering with my toe.

The weight of the box dragged at my bruised rib. Cursing at the delay, I administered a double kick before resting the burden on the window-sill to my right. When the woodwork had stopped shaking, the silence renewed itself.

I stood saying things to myself that were not complimentary with regard to Elaine's promptitude. If she wanted to check on who was knocking, there had now been ample time for her to do so. Perhaps she was nonplussed by the Land-Rover: she would have been expecting the Fiesta again. I backed off to where she could see me from an upper window.

'Elaine? It's me, Paul.'

After a moment I went forward once more. The left-hand side of the door was occupied by a wooden knob: as a matter of form I gave it a twist. Surprisingly, it released the catch, allowing the door to drift inwards. Stepping through, I banged the box down hard on the scullery table, hoping that a few things inside it would come apart. Despite all the noise, there was still no sign of the person for whom they were intended.

The scullery felt warm. An electric wall-heater was fully on, sending its influence across the mild chaos of the room. On the far end of the table sat the remnants of a snack: a crust or two of toast on an egg-scummed plate, and alongside it a cup two-thirds full of black coffee. I felt the china: it was cold. Near the plate stood a transistor radio. No sound was coming from it, but when I turned the 'off' switch it gave a final click of interment.

About to retrace my steps for the second box, I hesitated.

The internal door of the scullery was shut, yet something about it didn't seem right. My eye had picked up a movement, or my ear a sound . . . I couldn't be certain which. I went towards it, pausing a yard short. 'Elaine? Is that you?'

The inquiry echoed back into my teeth. In the silence that followed, I observed that the door was secured by an antiquated latch of wrought iron: a ringed bar that slotted into a groove. Reaching out, I pushed the bar up with a thumb. The metal yielded in a harsh clatter.

The door moved an inch towards me. About to help it

on its way, I felt the sudden pressure on my arm as it
came on at lightning speed, scything inwards to catch me a
dizzying blow on the temple. Amid a burst of coloured
sparks I was aware of a whirl of movement, a thrust against
my shoulder that sent me sprawling. I was in close com-
munion with an oak dresser near the door; crockery was
tumbling. Just as I was grabbing instinctively to save it,
the dresser itself fell on me.

The inside of the seashell was interesting. Veined blue and
gold, it contained a quantity of dust. This perplexed me.
The tide should have washed it clean by now.

Presently an answer suggested itself. It was not a conch
but the interior of my own skull, void, cavernous, resounding to my heartbeat. I considered this possibility. To an
extent it seemed valid, but there were question-marks. An
empty head suggested absence of thought. Such was not
the case: ideas, images, reflections were paddling before my
eyes like a flotilla of waterfowl. There must be more to it
than a vacant mind.

Once the realization dawned that what I was staring into
was neither shell nor skull, but the jagged-edged lower half
of a porcelain vase, I had the wit to raise my head from the
floor. Hard and malodorous, it was not the place to remain
for longer than was essential. Using an elbow, I levered
myself to a sitting position, drawing in breath sharply as a
keen edge dug into the butt of my hand. It belonged to a
handle of the vase, still attached to the upper half. About me
lay a scattering of other ceramic fragments. Memory stirred.

In a kneeling posture, I felt the throbbing in my head.

Presently I got a grip of something. It proved to be a
handle of one of the dresser drawers. The dresser, to my
mystification, had returned to an upright position. Had it
fallen on me? Something had. The throb was there to
remind me.

With the aid of the handle I got to my feet. The room lurched, recovered, reeled again, sent a wall flying against me. Using it as a back-support I edged towards the door latch, which was again in its socket. Abandoning caution, I knocked it up a second time and hauled the door open.

Beyond it lay an inner entrance hall with an open staircase climbing out of it. The light that filtered down from the landing above looked artificial. Stumbling across to the stair rail, I stood clutching the bottom post.

'Elaine!'

After a while I launched an ascent of the stairs. My shoes came down on the unpadded treads like hammers on six-inch nails: every decibel was torture. At the top, four doors led off from a narrow gallery. The one at the farther end stood ajar. Light from inside the room spilled along to the stairhead. When my head had stopped spinning from exertion I set course for the light-source, bumping from wall to guardrail as I staggered along.

With a knee, I thrust the door wide open. Much of the room was occupied by a large double bed, swamped by a rumpled, red-and-purple counterpane which spread also across part of the floor as if designed for a palace bridal chamber. On top of the counterpane lay a figure, face down. Most of it was concealed by a royal blue dressing-gown; the part that was not consisted largely of a familiar sprawl of red-gold hair, parts of which were less gold than crimson. If I hadn't known Elaine so well, I should have suspected her of using a tint. The fact that my entry had failed to arouse her suggested something else. Bending over her, I shook her by a shoulder.

'Can't you hear, Elaine? Are you drugged up or something?'

At that point I let go of her, because there was a stickiness between my fingers.

CHAPTER 7

'Your proper course was to call the CID immediately. It's for them to—'

'No phone,' I explained, 'at the farmhouse.'

'In that event,' said Police Constable Marsh, unfazed, 'you should've made direct for the nearest one you could find.'

'By the time I'd done that, it was quicker to drive back here and report to you.'

'How about your own phone? Don't you live just half a mile from Prior's?'

'Does it matter?' I demanded in exasperation. 'Maybe I wasn't thinking clearly. It only took me ten minutes to get here. Are they sending someone along?'

Marsh, who combined the appearance of a village bobby with the manner of a Cambridge don, smiled faintly in my direction. 'Generally speaking, Mr Hunt, the people at regional headquarters tend not to pigeonhole notifications of sudden death.' Accelerating into Parsons Lane, he pushed the Panda car to fifty through the bends, bringing me out in a clammy sweat: the second that morning. 'They're sending someone all right. Likely as not they'll beat us to it. You all right, sir? Not wanting to throw up?'

'Since you ask, I don't feel at the top of my form, but I think your upholstery's safe.'

'Sort of a delayed effect, these things can have.' Although he spoke with a knowing air, privately I questioned whether his direct experience of mortal violence was greatly more extensive than my own. 'Just when you think you've ridden it, back it comes to—Excuse me.'

A garbled message was being squawked from his radio. While he was answering I put my head back and shut my eyes, reopening them hastily as nausea and giddiness edged in on me. 'As I thought,' said Marsh complacently, restoring full attention to the lane ahead. 'They've a team there already. Save us the job of first exam. Can't say I was looking forward to that. Not a very pleasant spectacle, I dare say?'

I gulped. 'I'm trying not to think about it.'

He jerked a thumb at the glove compartment. 'Open that up, you'll find a flask. Help yourself.'

The brandy had no obvious beneficial effect, but taking swigs of it kept me occupied until we turned off to follow the track down to Prior's Farm. Another police car was parked in the yard. Pulling up alongside, Marsh scrambled out and made for the scullery door, turning before he got there to come back and supervise my emergence by placing a palm beneath my elbow. The gesture could have been supportive. 'They'll be wanting a statement from you. Feel up to that?'

'I've given you one.'

'Full details—the works. I'd be getting my thoughts together, sir, if I was in your shoes.'

Inside the scullery, he motioned me into a chair before advancing to the internal door, carefully avoiding the china shards that still lay strewn about the floor. He poked his head through the gap. 'Constable Bryan Marsh reporting,' he called powerfully.

A voice replied faintly. He came back. 'Long as they know we're here,' he remarked contentedly.

He leaned against the table. 'Catch sight of the instrument, did you?'

I looked at him blankly. 'Instrument?'

'Murder weapon. From what you've told me, I reckon

we can assume foul play. Hardly likely to have done it to herself, is she?'

'Unless she fell heavily against something.'

'Then bounced back on to the bed?' Marsh shook his head profoundly. 'We can rule out self-infliction, if I know anything. People don't normally peg out from bumping into the wardrobe.' He paused. 'She *was* a goner, sir, I take it? What convinced you?'

'The fact that she wasn't breathing.'

'Checked her pulse, did you?'

'Hardly seemed necessary. She was lying on her face and there was blood everywhere.'

'Must've given you a nasty turn.'

'To add to the one I'd had already.'

The constable leaned forward keenly. 'Yes. Now, this assault you say you underwent yourself. Was it—'

A stomping of feet on the stairs arrested him. He came to attention as a burly man of medium height, clad in a casual jacket and tartan slacks, entered from the hall, side-stepping the fragments. Marsh produced a salute of sorts. 'PC Bryan Marsh, sir, stationed at West Milldean. Death reported at ten fifty-three a.m. by Mr Paul Hunt here, finder of the body.'

Ignoring me, the newcomer stood massaging his scalp. 'Glad I don't have to live in one of these mediæval hell-holes. Too many jutting beams for my taste. I've already added to the blood-count, and I'm no Goliath.' His gaze swung my way. 'Mr . . . Hunt? You discovered the victim? Care to tell me about it?'

'Constable Marsh has the details.'

'Right, and Constable Marsh will be conveying those to me in due course . . . after he's explained what you both think you're up to, spreading yourselves over furniture at the scene of crime.' The constable's mouth fell open. His superior made for the outer door. 'Step outside with me for a moment, will you, Mr Hunt? Constable, you stay on the door. Try not to lean on it. Wouldn't want to eliminate every last trace, would we?'

'No, sir. I'm sorry.'

'So you damn well ought to be.' Pursuing me out to the yard, the detective brought his nostrils close to my mouth and took a sniff. 'Been imbibing, have we?'

'I had some brandy from the constable's flask. Felt a bit squiffy.'

His lips tightened. 'I see.' He shot a smouldering glance towards Marsh, now stationed at the scullery threshold. 'I'm DCI Steven Duke,' he informed me, turning back. 'Quite by chance, I and a colleague were in the neighbourhood on another matter when we got the call from headquarters, so we were here at the double. How long since you first stumbled upon the lady?'

I tried to recall. 'It's a bit hazy. I must have got here around ten, or a little before. Then I was out for a while. Around ten-thirty, it must have been.'

His forehead puckered. 'Out? What do you mean, you were out?'

'Somebody hit me.'

'Oh yes? Where?'

'Back of the head.'

'I mean *where*?'

'Inside there.' I nodded towards the scullery. 'Whoever it was came storming past as I was opening the internal door, and clocked me one.'

'The killer, presumably. Did you get a look?'

'No, sorry. It was just a blur of movement. I was knocked to one side against the dresser: then I passed out. When I came round, he'd gone.'

'So it was a man?'

'I'm just assuming.'

Indicating the police car, Chief Inspector Duke led me

over to it. With both of us packed inside, he said, 'Perilous to assume. But we'll skate round that for the minute. What I'm anxious to know, Mr Hunt, is just what you were doing here at Prior's Farm in the first place. Social call, was it?'

'No. I was making a delivery.'

Under his questioning I expanded on the background. Listening, he studied the farmhouse through the windscreen, as though sizing it up as the setting for a possible TV crime series. Many of his actions and mannerisms seemed to have been borrowed from the small screen, although beneath the slight exhibitionism lurked, I suspected, a shrewd grasp of basics. Before I had finished, two more police vehicles slewed into the yard to disgorge men and materials on to the gravel. Excusing himself, Duke climbed out to meet them, issued orders, vanished briefly into the farmhouse and then came back.

'So,' he observed, rejoining me inside the car. 'It all stemmed from these letters? The ones you were delivering on behalf of your friends.'

'That's what brought me here yesterday. Then the . . . the occupant and I got talking and she placed an order with me.'

'For supplies? Which you came along with this morning?'

'Right.'

'Up until yesterday, you'd not met her?'

'I'd no idea who was living here,' I said truthfully. 'Nobody had.'

'Someone must have had, surely?'

'What I mean is, she was something of a mystery figure to the village at large. Her name hadn't got about.'

'You don't happen to know her name?'

'Haven't a clue what she was calling herself.' Another reply of irreproachable accuracy. Duke eyed me for a moment before turning his attention broodingly to the activity surrounding the farmhouse. White tape was being employed to enclose an area embracing the yard and its approaches. A man holding a bag was applying dust to the scullery door and its frame; another with a camera was crouched over tyre tracks in the gravel, taking shots. Yet another car arrived to set down a tubby, white-haired individual carrying what looked like a medical case. Duke leapt out to accost him. They conversed briefly, and the latest arrival went inside.

The Chief Inspector returned. 'You'll be wanting to get back to your shop, Mr Hunt?'

'I'd appreciate it.'

'We can contact you there?'

'Or at home. Spring Cottage, half a mile along the lane in that direction. Constable Marsh knows.'

'I'm glad,' he said caustically, 'there's something Constable Marsh is aware of. I'll get him to run you back.'

'Thank you, Chief Inspector.'

'Not planning to absent yourself from the district, were you, in the course of the next few days? Early holiday or something?'

'Shopkeepers,' I explained kindly, 'don't take holidays.'

Trade at the Pantiles that afternoon was brisk.

By some remarkable convergence of inclination, villagers by the dozen who had found themselves in no need of post-prandial refreshment for many weeks rediscovered their thirsts and appetites and came into the teashop to attend to them. While there, they took care to inquire after my health before alluding casually to vague rumours they had heard of 'some sort of bother up at Prior's' and voicing due astonishment upon learning that I was in a position to contribute to the general fund of knowledge relating to the incident in question. For several frustrating hours, Gillian was kept pinned to the kitchen range, producing additional scones and rock cakes when all her instincts must have been shrieking at her to take me to one side and assume the role of privileged confidante. I made a mental note to give her twenty minutes of my time at the end of the day, exclusively for this purpose. It was important to stay on the right side of my assistant. I had a feeling I should be needing her more than ever.

Prominent among the customers was Bridget, on her way home by car from a visit with the Church Fellowship to the gardens of Havington House in Lower Marling, the next village but two. At four o'clock she strode in, all scarlet cheeks and protruding teeth.

'Phwat's *this* I hear? When I said deliver a message, I didn't mean frighten the poor woman to death.'

'I'm the one who was terrified.'

'Give me a pot of tea,' she commanded, 'and one of those gooey, chocolatey things with fudge at both ends. And let's have all the gory details.'

'You've been twelve miles away,' I remarked, 'since early this morning. How on earth did you get to hear about it?'

'Had to call in on old Mrs Guttridge. She'd heard from—'

'Say no more. There's not a lot else I can tell you, Bridget. I found her body, that's all. The cops took over from there.'

'You sound extraordinarily cheerful about it. In your place, I'd have been under twenty-four-hour sedation.'

'I've a teashop to run. Gill, a pot of our best Darjeeling for Mrs Sheeney, and a caramel slice. Now then, Bridget. What is it you want to know?'

She glared. 'Everything, of course. Patty will never forgive me if I can't come across with the works.'

'If I were in a position to tell you chapter and verse, the CID boys would be out of a job.' I offered a sketchy description of my discovery of Elaine plus a few snippets of the subsequent investigation, as far as I had witnessed it. Bridget looked dissatisfied.

'Phwat about the weapon? Did they find that?'

'I wasn't told. Don't even know what they were looking for.'

'A blunt instrument,' Bridget suggested with relish.

I poked her through to the tea-room. 'Sit at the corner table,' I ordered, 'and discuss it with Miss Jefferson there, if you must. I've more mundane things to attend to.' A quick scan of the other customers showed me that some spirited cross-talk was going on: not for months had such a mood of *joie de vivre* alighted upon the Pantiles tea-tables. 'It seems to take a violent death,' I murmured, 'to bring out the positive in people. In the ordinary way, this lot would be slumped in glum silence, preoccupied with their buttered toast.'

'In the ordinary way,' boomed Bridget, 'they wouldn't be here at all. Talking of toast, I think I'll have some. I'm quite peckish.' She went to join Miss Jefferson, who shrank visibly at her approach. I returned to the shop to convey her additional order to Gillian. Another customer had arrived and was waiting by the till. It was the schoolteacher. My greeting contained a touch of irony.

'Not often we see you in here. Something in particular you were after?'

'A birthday gift,' she said briskly. 'Anything in the eatable category . . . offbeat, if possible. For a child of seven.'

'One of your flock?'

'Who else?'

Echoes of challenge hung in the reply. Not wishing to get into another loaded exchange, I put on a show of fingering the gems of my collection. 'This package is quite popular. Coconut ice and truffle, with a little cylinder of chocolate beans — see? After you've eaten the beans you can use the cylinder to keep pound coins in. Do seven-year-olds handle that sort of money, these days?'

'Some of them keep fivers in their blouse pockets. You'd be surprised.'

'Evidently. I'm out of touch.' Wrapping the confectionery, I took the cash she handed over. Accepting change, she met my eye.

'Feeling better?'

'Um . . . better than what?'

'Bridget said you were quite shaken up.'

'You've seen her?'

Angela looked puzzled. 'We spoke on the phone.'

'When was that?'

She gave her hair a nervy tug. 'A day or so ago. Is that relevant, at all?'

I said cautiously, 'I think possibly we're talking at cross-purposes. You're referring to my inadvertent detour into a ravine?'

'Yes. Why? Have you crashed again since then?'

'In a mannner of speaking. Against an oak dresser. You've not heard?'

She looked at me dumbly. I gave her a three-sentence outline of more recent events. 'That's what I thought you'd come in to quiz me about. Everyone else has.'

'I've been stuck in class all afternoon. None of the children could have heard, otherwise I'd have known soon enough. How dreadful.'

'It wasn't pleasant.'

'Not your lucky week.'

'In some ways,' I agreed.

'I expect you don't want to talk about it.'

'If you want to know more,' I suggested, 'you'll find Bridget through there, grazing on her way home. She's fully briefed.'

Angela went to the dividing door and glanced through

before returning to the counter. 'She also looks fully occupied. I think I'll leave her to it. Thanks for the gift idea. Hope you have better luck from now on.'

'It's an odd thing,' I told her, 'but I've a feeling I might be going to.'

Our eyes met again, briefly. 'Nice to be optimistic,' she said, and left the shop.

Emerging from the tea-room with a tray on each arm, Gillian said admiringly, 'Ever so good with the kids she is, they say, that one. Was she asking about the murder?'

'Strangely enough, she wasn't. She hadn't heard.'

'My! You'd think she would've. Kids usually get to hear, one way or another. Beats me how, but they do.' She vanished into the kitchen. I followed her through.

'Anything I can take?'

'Only if you feel up to it, Mr Hunt.'

'I'm not a physical wreck. In fact, I'm feeling much better.'

'That's good,' Gillian said disbelievingly. 'Had a lot to put up with, haven't you, just lately?'

'Those ready to go? Pass 'em over.' Seizing the freshly loaded trays, I carried them into the tea-room, parried a few more questions, bartered further insults with Bridget and cleared a table or two before returning to the shop and taking a rest on the seat behind the counter. I had not been dissembling to Gillian: mentally and bodily I felt greatly improved. Better, in fact, than I had for several years. At the same time, a desire for sleep had overtaken me. A lull seemed to have occurred in the customer stream. Closing my eyes, I leaned back, focusing my mind on the more upbeat aspects of the situation, trying to blank out the starker images of the morning. Drowsiness swam over me. An hour to closing time. Trading flourished. Life was good. From the tea-room, the conversational drone had a sedating influence.

The clang of the doorbell jolted me out of slumber.

Although the face and burly build of the man who came in were familiar, for a moment I couldn't place him. Then he opened his mouth, and I could. 'Hoped I might find you here, Mr Hunt. That your Land-Rover parked outside?'

'Yes. I always keep it there.' Why, I wondered foggily, should a DCI concern himself with a possible parking misdemeanour? 'Should I shift it? I didn't think it was in anybody's way.'

'Spare us a few minutes?' His intonation rose at the end, but it wasn't a question. Detaching myself from the chair, I yawned, knuckled the sleep out of my eyes.

'Don't tell me. You now want a signed statement?'

'I want you to come outside.' Holding the door, Duke waited for me to pass through, then joined me on the footway. Along by the vehicle, the back of which was open, a uniformed sergeant stood guard in a posture which gained elements of greater rigidity at our approach. Nearby, one or two shoppers were taking an overt interest in proceedings. Halting by the tailgate, Duke beckoned me to his side.

'Something here I'd like you to take a look at, Mr Hunt. If you wouldn't mind.'

'Look,' I said, 'I realize this is technically a yellow band area, but I've always—'

'Recognize this, sir?' He was showing me something wrapped in clear polythene which he had taken from the floor of the Land-Rover. I gave it an uncomprehending stare.

'It's a carriage clock.'

'I'm aware of what it is. Have you seen it before?'

'Should I have?'

'I'm asking.'

'I've seen dozens like it. Brass, I imagine. Where's it from?'

He pointed into the vehicle. 'There.'

'You mean you found it there? It's nothing to do with me. I don't carry clocks about with me. Anyway, what were you doing, searching my—'

'You're saying you didn't know it was there?'

'Of course not. I've never even owned one.'

'Ever given one to somebody?'

'I'd need to think back . . .'

'Be doing that, would you, while we're taking you to the incident room. There's a few questions I'd like to put to you.'

'Hey, wait a bit. I can't just leave the shop.'

'It won't run off. You can leave word with your girl. Oh, before we start back . . .'

Upending the clock, he showed me its base. Engraved on the casing were the words *Elaine, with all my affection, from Paul*. The Chief Inspector waited for a moment before adding, 'Does that stir any kind of memory?'

I shook my head.

'You're certain? Don't rush at it, Mr Hunt. Be clear in your mind.'

'If it meant anything to me, I'd know, wouldn't I?'

'One would be entitled to think so.' Turning the clock the right way up, he inspected it critically from a new angle. 'Prime condition,' he remarked, 'except that it's been messed up a little, just recently. Fairly stained, it was, when we came upon it ten minutes ago. We've cleaned it up a bit. Taken off most of the blood that was clinging to it, kept it for analysis. Outcome of that could be revealing, Mr Hunt, wouldn't you say?'

CHAPTER 8

After nearly an hour the Chief Inspector was called away, leaving me to contemplate the interior of the police van in which a makeshift incident room had been set up in the farmhouse yard. Unheated, it had started me shivering as soon as I entered; I still had less than total control over my muscles.

The coffee given to me out of a jug was not helping. It tasted like one of Bridget's worst excesses, with the added defect that no sweetener was available, although someone had gone off to find some and failed to return. The van was equipped with a couple of small tables bearing portable telephones, a desktop computer, and a few other items of equipment that looked clever. While I was trying to guess at their functions, Duke came back. His expression, too, was giving nothing away. He reclaimed his chair, facing mine at an angle.

'So. You deny ever giving the clock to Elaine Turner? You weren't acquainted with the lady?'

I gestured. 'There must be half a million Pauls in the south of England. Any one of them could have had that inscribed.'

'Answer the question, please.'

'For the sixth time, I didn't.'

'Know her?'

'Or present her with the damn clock. I came here this morning to deliver supplies. It was a business deal. Nothing more. Can't you accept that?'

'Believe me, I'm trying. Problem is . . .' He wrinkled his nose, squinted, sniffed. 'There are other factors that need taking into account. In the first place, if you know nothing of that particular timepiece—and it's a handsome job of work, well crafted, solid—the question that then arises is, how did it get into the back of your vehicle?'

'I've given you a perfectly logical explanation. Whoever killed Elaine . . . Elaine Turner stowed it inside there while I was out cold in the scullery.'

'To incriminate you?'

'Obviously. What could have been simpler? There was my Land-Rover with its back open: all the killer had to do was throw the clock inside as he went past.'

'Why didn't you spot it when you came out?'

'For Heaven's sake! I'd just been slugged; I'd just found a dead body; I was on my way to report it. Investigating the back of my wagon wasn't uppermost in my mind at the time.'

Duke meditated. 'If you're not drinking any more of that,' he said finally, reaching for my coffee cup, 'we'll have it out of the way.' Inserting a pencil through the handle, he slid the cup to the other end of the table. 'Any theories of your own, Mr Hunt, as to the identity of the culprit?'

'I just wish I had. It might have been anyone.'

'Male, though, in your opinion?'

'I don't see that a woman could have hit me like that, hard enough to put me out for several minutes.'

'Not without using the clock on you, perhaps. Why didn't he or she use the clock?'

'Maybe they did.'

Duke shook his head. 'That dent in your flesh is consistent with a fist or an elbow. The clock would have broken your skin, to say the least.'

'OK, so it was bare knuckles. The reason being,' I added, suddenly inspired, 'that I was a handy scapegoat. So the killer didn't want to use the same weapon on me that he'd used on the woman. That would have lifted suspicion from me.'

'What you're saying,' Duke said after further pondering, 'is that he hoped it would be deduced that you'd had some kind of a tussle with the lady upstairs, in the course of which you knocked your head against something? And subsequently lost consciousness, having first killed her with the clock and then staggered downstairs to fall against the dresser? Something like that?'

'Sounds ramshackle,' I conceded, 'but then he didn't have much time to fabricate it all, did he? He had to think and act fast.' A thought occurred to me. 'Incidentally, what led you to search my vehicle? Not an anonymous tip-off, by any chance?'

He surveyed me tolerantly. 'If you were inquiring into a murder, Mr Hunt, and the finder of the body spun you a tale about meeting the killer on his way out . . . you'd want to eliminate various possibilities, would you not? Especially if the murder weapon was missing from the scene. We'd have been failing in our duty if we hadn't searched the vehicle you arrived in.' He rubbed his nose. 'Not, frankly, that I expected to come across anything of a suspicious nature. You'd have had plenty of time to dispose of it.'

'Well, exactly! You don't imagine that I'd have left the thing lying around inside the load space, then left the Land-Rover parked in the main street with all the doors unlocked? Talk about inviting trouble.'

'Don't you ever lock the doors?'

'Not when I leave it in the village. I've never had anything pinched. You haven't answered the question.'

'I'm doing the asking, in case you've forgotten. But since we're on the subject, I could venture the suggestion that you did so for this very reason.'

'What reason?'

'To enable you to claim that you'd been set up.'

I sat staring at him. 'Sounds a bit over-subtle to me.'

'For all I know, Mr Hunt, you may be a remarkably

subtle man. You do strike me, in fact, as reasonably bright.'

'Thank you.'

'Scarcely the type I'd have expected to find running a teashop in a somewhat remote Hampshire village.'

'What type would you label me as?'

The finger-rubbing transferred itself from his nose to his chin. 'Oh . . . I don't know. Executive? Put you in a dark suit, clutching a briefcase, and I could see you taking far-reaching decisions on the hoof, answering to shareholders . . . all that. Been in your present occupation long?'

'I'm quite sure you've asked around already. So you'll doubtless know that I took over the Pantiles about eighteen months ago, on the recommendation of a friend of mine who reckoned I could make a go of it.'

'Where were you, previous to that?'

'London area.'

'Uh-huh. London's a big place.'

'Hampstead,' I said reluctantly. 'I worked there for a number of years.'

'How old are you now?'

'Thirty-two.'

'Was that your first job?'

'Yes. Before that I was up at university.'

'Oxbridge?' he speculated.

'East Anglia.'

'That where you hail from?'

'Lincoln.'

'Nice city. I've a brother-in-law, lives around there.' The Chief Inspector drifted momentarily into abstraction. 'Bit odd, really,' he resumed abruptly. 'Elaine Turner was formerly in the Hampstead area.'

'You don't say?'

'She lived in Highgate.' He cocked an eyebrow. 'You could easily have run into her.'

'I used to mix with a lot of people.'

'Mmm, I suppose you would. What were you up to in Hampstead, Mr Hunt, might I ask?'

'Up to?'

'Your job. Your position.'

'I was a fund manager with a firm of financial advisers.'

'Dished out sound advice, did they?'

'I wasn't really there long enough to find out.'

'Grew tired of the rat-race? Dropped out to West Milldean?'

'Maybe I just wanted to be my own boss.'

'Don't we all?' Duke's facial tissue went into folds as he considered his own rhetorical question. 'I wonder, you know, whether something of the same sort might account for Miss Turner's apparent self-exile to this part of the world?'

'You're hardly in a position to ask her.'

'Sadly, we're not. Does that please you, Mr Hunt?'

'What?'

'I thought I detected a note of faint satisfaction in your voice. Forgive me if I'm wrong.'

'It's of no consequence to me, one way or the other.'

'I don't quite see how you can claim that. Like it or not, your destiny's tied up with hers for the moment. Let me ask you once again: up until yesterday, Miss Turner's existence meant nothing to you? You're adamant about that?'

I stood up. 'The thing I'm adamant about is that you either arrest me or let me get back to the shop. Am I free to leave, or what?'

He sat with arms folded, surveying me.

'You'll be wanting a ride back to the village?'

'Not necessary. I can walk from here to my cottage.'

'But your vehicle's still parked in the main street.'

'I'll cadge a lift from someone, pick it up this evening. Please don't go to any more trouble on my account.'

'Oh, it's not on your account,' he assured me. 'It's ours.

Also Miss Turner's, of course. One has to be candid about that.'

The lounge bar of the Stag was dimly lit, warm, full of a conversational buzz which seemed to falter briefly as I came in. Possibly it was my imagination. I asked Rosemary, the bar lady, for a Scotch and ginger. Her smile of welcome was as broad as usual. About to pay for the drink, I was tapped on the shoulder.

'Allow me,' requested the voice of Roger Ashby. 'You're about due for a break.'

'How do you mean?'

'Aren't you the guy who stumbles over lifeless torsos? That must warrant a free drink.'

'Finding the body,' I said bleakly, 'is the least of my problems. Practically being accused of putting it there is what stings a little.'

Ashby guffawed. 'Well, if you must be in the wrong place at the wrong . . .' He gave me a closer look. 'You're not serious?'

'I'm not, but the cops seem to be. I've just been the guinea-pig for one of their latest exercises in third degree.'

'My dear chap.' Ashby clicked several fingers at the bar lady. 'Rosemary, line up a chaser for whatever Paul is having and shove it all on the slate. Did you catch that? Paul reckons—'

'No need to spread it around,' I muttered.

'Spreading is the last thing it'll need,' he said with brutal realism. 'Seeing it's going to be all over the district by this time tomorrow, you might just as well cash in, exploit the situation. What makes 'em imagine *you* did it, for God's sake?'

'The murder weapon was allegedly found in my wagon.'

Ashby and Rosemary swapped glances. Snapping open

a second bottle of ginger ale, the bar lady said tentatively, 'What was it?'

'A clock.'

Ashby succeeded in half-suppressing another paroxysm. 'So, he clocked her one. Classic example of a noun employed as verb ... Sorry. This is serious. Allegedly, you say? You're disputing that it could have been found there?'

'Oh, I think quite probably it was. I'm not accusing the police of planting it. But I'm perfectly certain it was planted by someone else.'

'Like the killer?'

'To me, it's so obvious. There I was at the scene of the crime, tailor-made for incrimination. The Fuzz don't see it that way.'

'They've let you go,' Rosemary pointed out comfortingly. 'They must realize they can't make it stand up.'

'She's right, you know.' Ashby eyed me for a moment. 'To make it stick, they'd need proof of motivation, aside from anything else. What motive could you possibly have?'

'Robbery. Lust.'

'Was she a looker?'

'She was a knockout,' I said after a short pause.

Ashby lifted his gaze to the bar ceiling. 'Now he tells me. If I'd known ... But we won't got into that now. Well, my son, at least you've got yourself in a scrape over somebody worthwhile, from the sound of it. If you're going to become part of a murder inquiry, you might as well spruce up your macho image while you're at it. No sense in—'

'Pipe down, Roger,' admonished Rosemary, a no-nonsense woman with a tender streak. 'Paul's very upset, and so would you be. It's not nice to be victimized. I remember Freddie and me, eight or nine years back. We had this fire at the last pub we were keeping, over at Great Fallowdean, and the company as good as accused us of starting it ourselves, on purpose, to cover up losses in the accounting.

Quite nasty about it, they got, for a while. Until we were able to . . . well, that's another story. The thing is, I know how Paul must feel. It's the sense of injustice, isn't it, dear? All manner of things you feel you want to say, only you can't think of the words.'

'I can think of a few,' I said grimly. 'By tomorrow, after a sleepless night, I'll probably have marshalled quite a lot.'

'That's the spirit.'

''Evening, Mr Hunt. Buy you that drink I owe you?'

The man who had joined us was short and Pickwickian, with side whiskers of a feline reach and rigidity that were balanced by a famine of cranial thatch. 'Cyril Blake,' he introduced himself, noting the blankness of my expression. 'Starks Farm. We spoke on the phone. What's it to be? Same as you've got there?'

'They seem to be forming a queue,' I said, shaking his small, doughlike hand. 'I'm on whisky-macs, but I don't think I should—'

'Rosemary—another Scotch for Mr Hunt.' Blake's whiskers quivered. 'Having done our best to drown him in stream water, we may as well finish him off with the distilled variety. Still feeling none the worse, I trust?'

'He's feeling very bruised,' Rosemary informed him, 'but not because of anything young Kevin did to him. Since then—'

'Other troubles have befallen me,' I said swiftly, arranging the third whisky glass alongside its predecessor on the bar counter. 'No need to bore you with them. How's the farming world?'

He grimaced. 'Don't ask. These new EC regulations . . .'

With a murmured excuse, Ashby drifted further along the counter to involve himself with a couple I didn't recognize. Rosemary went to serve them. Breaking off in mid-sentence, Blake eyed me perciently. 'You don't really want to know all this, do you? These other troubles you mentioned just now—anything I might be able to help out with?'

'Only if you've a considerable pull with the top brass of the CID.'

He tugged at the collar of his purple shirt. 'Apart from Bryan Marsh, the only coppers I know personally . . . You're entangled with the law?'

'It's nothing. Some stupid misunderstanding. It'll blow over.'

Blake edged nearer. 'Nothing to do with that odd business you were telling me about? The noises in your cottage?'

'That's still a thorn in my flesh,' I admitted, seizing thankfully upon the diversion. 'They're still occurring and I can't seem to nail 'em down. It's partly why I'm here this evening. Keeps me out of the damn place as long as possible. I'm a refugee from the supernatural.'

'There's always a straightforward explanation, in my experience. TV still switching itself on and off?'

'No, I've put a stop to that. I now disconnect plug from socket before going to bed.'

'But the rest of it is as bad as ever?'

'Worse.'

'Extraordinary.' Blake peered around. 'Look here, let me reintroduce you to young Kevin. He might be able to suggest something. Knowledgeable young spark, he is, in his own way: clued-up in sound effects. Organizes the weekly discos for the Young Farmers' League. See if he can put his finger on anything. He's just through there, drinking with his mates. Kev! Spare us a minute?'

Riley pushed a way through to us, via the archway that connected the lounge with the public bar. To his faintly embarrassed smile I responded with a grin and an outstretched hand. 'Got that tow-rope handy, Kevin? I've a feeling I could well be driving into another ditch by the time I get out of here.'

'I'll stand by, Mr Hunt.'

'Our friend here,' Blake told his employee, 'has a problem. He'll describe it to you.'

The young farm-hand was a good listener, saving his questions until the end. 'Any other equipment in your cottage, aside of the TV?'

'Not a thing.'

'Stereo system? Home computers? Cassette recorders?'

'Nothing of that species.'

'Central heating?'

'All I have is a couple of electric fires.'

'Keep 'em plugged in?'

'Only when they're in use.'

'Immersion water heater?'

'Yes, I've got one of those.'

'Where's the cylinder?'

'Um . . . inside the airing cupboard on the landing.'

'Have it put in, did you?'

'No. It was there when I came.'

'May be getting on a bit, then. If the heater's packing up,' explained Riley earnestly, 'you could start getting noises. Once the element casing perishes, see, then you get direct contact with the water in the cylinder. Then . . . *whoo-oosh*. Like Concorde going over.'

'If it were that,' said Blake, looking impressed if sceptical, 'wouldn't the thing have disintegrated by now?'

Riley shrugged. 'Just an idea.'

'Besides,' I said, 'why only at night?'

'When d'you switch on the immersion?'

'Before I turn in,' I confessed. 'I get the cheap rate.'

Riley looked a little pleased with himself. 'Could be summat like that, I reckon.'

Blake surveyed him with a touch of paternal pride. 'Any way you could check?'

'Need to have it out, take a look.'

'How about it, Mr Hunt? Paul, very well. Can Kevin trot along some time, give it the once-over? Do it for the price of a pint, won't you, lad?'

'It's extremely good of you. I would be grateful. But I don't want to impose.'

'No bother. Kevin's got his own transport. One evening next week?'

'If you're sure.' Privately I questioned whether the cause could possibly be something as relatively inanimate as an immersion heater: at the same time, I was desperate enough to grasp at straws. And Riley did seem to know what he was talking about. We fixed upon a date for him to call in, and I stood him a pint of lager: payment in advance. After that the evening became a little confused. At one point, Ashby and another man were back with us, conducting an uproarious debate upon a topic that remained an enigma to me, bellowing with laughter and punching one another. I bought a further round of drinks. The atmosphere of the lounge became hot, smoke-laden, deafening. The cherubic features of Cyril Blake acquired a moist patina, melding eventually with those of the others into a shadowy mass, roaring at me. Since I could separate no sense from any of it, there seemed no point in remaining; but from where I was standing the precise location of the exit was unclear. Arms were helping me along. At the door, I pivoted to wave good night to the room at large and to confirm, hazily, that what lateral vision had been telling me for some while was indeed the case: Angela, the school-teacher, was seated on a bar stool chatting with Ashby in the hubbub. Feeling strangely downcast, I let myself be assisted into the keener air outside, and from there into the front passenger seat of the Land-Rover. Somebody else was taking the wheel.

'Can't have you forfeiting your licence,' said the voice of

Cyril Blake, swinging us dizzily out of the car park. 'You've enough—'

At this point I lost all track of events. Later, an eternity later, I was in bed with the room circling.

CHAPTER 9

'Golly, Mr Hunt. You look a bit rough.'

'Please keep your voice down, Gillian. No need to shout.'

'I'm talkin' in a whisper. Did they knock you around?'

'Did who knock me around?'

'The police. They say, if you don't tell 'em what they want to hear, they knock you around.'

A shaft of sunlight from above the roof of the supermarket dealt me a blow between the eyes. 'Shall we get inside? I don't think I'm altogether in the mood for sunny spells and bright intervals. Unlock the door, Gill, there's a love. I can't remember which pocket my keys are in.'

'If you ask me, they've been knocking you around. You want to complain, Mr Hunt, to the Civil Rights people. They'd soon put a stop to it. Police've got no right to go knocking people around. My dad says . . .'

Gillian's voice and body faltered to a standstill. Behind her on the doorstep of the Pantiles, I said faintly, 'Get a move on. I want to get out of the glare.'

Her answer was a high-pitched cry of distress. I said irritably, 'Now what's the matter?'

'I never left it like this. What's gone on here, then?'

Thrusting past her, I stood surveying the shop's interior. 'We've been done.'

'Eh?'

'Someone's broken in. They've turned the lot over.'

Gillian inhaled with a hiss. 'Crikey, so they have. Did

you ever see such a mess? Oh, Mr Hunt. Look, they even tore the packets open.' She pointed distractedly to the chocolate wrappings strewn across the floor.

'Maybe they had a sweet tooth.' I moved forward to make the futile gesture of retrieving cardboard boxes from the heap of tangled wreckage that had been dumped behind the counter. Stabs of pain darted through my head. I subsided with a moan against the till, the only sizeable object still in place. Gillian dabbed at my arm.

'Soon have it tidied up, Mr Hunt. All we need to do—'

'No, leave it. Don't touch anything. Get on the phone, will you, Gill? See if you can contact PC Marsh. If not, leave a message. I'd better be taking a look round the back.'

Fighting off a sick headache, I went through to the kitchen. Gillian's treasured array of pots, pans and implements lay in various corners, some of them battered hopelessly out of shape. Store cupboards had been gutted, their contents dispersed and trodden around the floor. One cupboard had been torn from the wall and smashed. After examining the rear door I went back into the shop.

'They broke in from the yard,' I informed Gillian, whose index finger was making furious stabs at the telephone dial. 'Must have swarmed over the wall. Don't go in there yet, love. It'll break your heart.'

'Constable Marsh there, please? Ta.' She covered the mouthpiece. 'You wanta have a look at the tea-room, Mr Hunt. Just you go an' take a look.'

'I don't think I do.' But I went anyway, and saw the worst for myself. When I returned, Gillian was hanging up. 'No luck?'

'His wife's putting out a call. He's on early duty at the school crossing.' Gillian gazed at me in despair. 'What we going to do, Mr Hunt? Can't serve anybody, can we, without chairs and tables? How will it—'

'First,' I interrupted, 'we put the CLOSED sign back in the

window . . . if we can find it. Wait, I've a better idea. Will you do something else for me, Gill? Find a bit of card or something, print on it CLOSED TEMPORARILY DUE TO BREAK-IN, then stick it up somewhere outside. Got anything to write with?'

She peered about miserably. 'See what I can find . . .'

Returning to the kitchen, I found that the electric kettle we kept under the sink for emergencies had had the spout wrenched off it. Adding it to the casualties already littering the floor, I leaned against the range and tried to assemble my thoughts. There were, I suspected, things that I should have been doing. For the moment it was easier just to stand there, staring into space. Presently the door opened and Gillian peered through, blinking at sight of the devastation.

'He's here, Mr Hunt.'

'Who's here?'

'Constable Marsh. Wants to ask you some things.'

Marsh squeezed past her. 'Not your week, is it, Mr Hunt? Got any ideas on this?'

'Yes. But they're not printable. Have you?'

'Tearaways,' he said with conviction. 'Did much the same to the King's Head at Misselton last week. Going around, probably. Louts with nothing better to do. Keep cash in the till overnight, do you?'

'Luckily, never. It goes into the night safe along the street.'

He scribbled a note. 'According to young Gill here, they came in round the back?'

'Take a look,' I invited him.

While he was nosing about the yard, I dialled my insurance company's helpline and spoke to a sympathetic female voice. 'You're in luck, Mr Hunt,' it advised me. 'We've someone in your area right now. He can be with you in half an hour. You'll be wanting to straighten things up as soon as possible?'

'That would help.'

'It's a Mr Saunders. Wait until he's had a look at the damage, then when the police are gone—get the case number from them, by the way—you can start tidying. My pleasure. Happy to oblige.'

In a harsh world, her soft professionalism did wonders for my headache. Revitalized, I went outside to view Gillian's literary accomplishment. Neatly blocked out in green ink, the message I had dictated had been Sellotaped to a pane of the window by the street entrance. Notwithstanding the omission of AR from TEMPORARILY, it was a workmanlike job. Adjoining shops were starting to open up. I wandered next door. Geoff, the family butcher, greeted me with a look of introspective concern from behind his joints.

'Hear you've taken a bit of a pasting. Make off with anything, did they?'

'Not to my knowledge. Just an orgy of destruction, by the look of it. No sign of anything here?'

'I'm happy to say there's not. Mind you, we've steel mesh over the plate glass, front and back. Take a bit of hacking through, that.'

'My place was obviously the easier option.' Through the window I caught sight of PC Marsh emerging into the street. 'Talk to you later, Geoff.' I went outside to rejoin the constable. 'Finished already?'

'Lad from the plainclothes brigade should be along shortly. He'll do a bit of forensic stuff. Must be off on my rounds. Kept up the insurance, have you? Pay for some smart new furniture, I reckon. Not that the old lot . . . well, you know what I mean. Week from now, Mr Hunt, you'll be back to better than normal. Hey, Gill?'

''Spect you're right, Mr Marsh,' she said dully.

We watched him purr off in his Panda. 'Resounding support,' I remarked, 'from all sides. Where can I get a cup of good, black coffee?'

'I'll fetch you some, Mr Hunt.'

With a purposeful air she set off for the supermarket, four doors along. The under-manager there was reputed to be her second cousin. As she vanished through its doors, a BMW saloon came at speed into sight and earshot, its driver peering up at the shop frontages. Reaching the Pantiles, he drew over and braked vigorously. 'Mr Hunt?' he inquired, leaping out.

'That's me. You'll be . . . ?'

'Les Saunders, loss adjuster, Fireburg Insurance plc. Hear you've had visitors.'

'What kept you?'

He smiled smugly. 'Not always as prompt as this, I don't mind telling you. Happens I was already in the neighbourhood. Blaze at Rootley Manor. So when they contacted me from base I was able to come straight here.'

'You're more than welcome. Step right in.'

About to follow him inside, I was honked from another car which wavered, wobbled, changed course and threw its tyre-walls with reckless violence against the kerbstone before lurching to a halt. The tragic countenance of the Rector gazed out.

'My dear boy! I've just heard. Is it bad?'

'Hardly what you'd call godly, Edgar. Who did you pick it up from?'

'I've just called in at the post office. Muriel there had got it from Mrs Pemberton, who spotted your notice as she came past a few minutes ago. Did they get their hands on anything of value?'

'There was nothing worth pinching. Now there's even less. I'm waiting for the CID now.'

'Think they'll be any help?'

'I doubt it. Why?'

The Rector looked profound. 'You seem to be having

more than your fair allocation of trial, just lately. Scarcely the handiwork of the Lord, perhaps?'

'Is there something you're trying to tell me, Edgar?'

'Actually I'm asking. You don't think it's possible you're being troubled by . . . shall we say, a tormented spirit?'

'You mean a poltergeist or something?'

'One should keep an open mind,' he said severely, 'on such matters. That's what I try to do. And I'll tell you something else: I do a very good line in exorcisms, should it come to the point. Do bear that in mind, won't you?'

'I will,' I said gravely. 'Thanks, Edgar. A positive contribution, if I may say so.'

'Well, I just thought I'd mention it. Meanwhile, we'll remember you in our prayers on Sunday. How's the other mucky business going, by the way?'

'The homicidal accusations department? I'll keep you informed. Prayer may not be enough.'

'A lot of nonsense,' he snorted. 'They should focus on finding the killer, not sidetrack themselves molesting innocent citizens. Chin up, Paul. Remember what I said. You know where to find me.'

The car pitched off in the direction of the church. Gillian came back, clutching a Thermos flask.

'You're to drink it while it's hot, Mr Hunt. Buck you right up, this will. My cousin made it himself.'

My hope that her relative had contrived to avoid the family curse in the realm of coffee-blending proved to be a vain one. To spare Gillian's feelings, I waited until she was occupied by other things inside the shop before surreptitiously emptying the flask's contents over the debris behind the counter; I was confident that it would make no perceptible difference to the chaos. Saunders, pocket tape-recorder in hand, joined us from the tea-room.

'Made a job of it, didn't they? Shame about some of those chairs. Early Edwardian style, quite collectable nowadays.

This lead to the kitchen?' He strolled through. Gillian blinked after him.

'Who's he, when he's at home with his boots fastened?'

'Bloke from the insurance,' I explained. 'He has to evaluate the damage before I can claim. Here's somebody else.'

The man from the CID had arrived. Announcing himself tersely as DC Thompson, he joined Saunders in the kitchen to dust for prints. I filled in the time by half-heartedly compiling, with Gillian's eloquent help, a list of items that had been shattered. On his return, Thompson gave tongue to pessimism.

'All insured, was it?'

'Yes. What are the chances?'

'Chances?'

'Of nailing them.'

'Thin. Not a lot to go on.'

'So you think they're quite likely to get away with it?'

The detective studied me. 'Much here worth lifting?'

'Not unless you're hooked on jelly beans.'

'Makes you query the motivation, then.'

'How do you mean, exactly?'

He shrugged. 'You do seem to be upsetting people lately, don't you, sir? Personal assault one day: violation of premises the next. Been walking under ladders, have we?'

I gave myself a moment to reply. 'You're not implying I rigged this break-in to support my version of events at Prior's Farm?'

He ignored the question. 'We'll be in touch, Mr Hunt. I'll let you have the case number. Start clearing up if you want to. I've done all I want.'

'I bet he has,' Gillian sniffed in the wake of his departure. 'Snooty young so-and-so. Wouldn't trust him to take the paw-prints off me pet rabbit. Make a start on this mess, then, shall we?'

'Let's just wait for the insurance man.'

Saunders reappeared presently, wiping his fingers on a tissue. 'All done. Should be no problems with the claim. I'll be on my way. Another fire at Ellchester. Busy morning. Way I like it, to be honest.' With an affable nod, divided equally between us, he made for the street. The BMW took off in a discreet howl of rubber. I sagged briefly at the shoulders before taking a grip on myself.

'OK, Gill. If we dump the worst of it out in the yard, we might be able to open up by this afternoon. Let's give it a go.'

Leaving the kitchen to her, I spent an hour reassembling the shop; then, bracing myself, I went through to the tea-room. Bad as it looked, some of the furniture, I discovered, was retrievable. Legs needed replacing in sockets, cross-members in joints, but with the aid of a hammer and a screwdriver I was able to restore enough chairs and tables to serviceable condition to bring an early reopening within the bounds of possibility. The walls and flooring of the room had escaped largely unmarked. To my relief, only one of Sandra's pictures seemed to have drawn the attention of the vandals. Depicting a local landmark, Bobdean Manor, it had been ripped from its frame and torn almost neatly in halves. Rolling up the two sections carefully, I took them out to the Land-Rover, then returned to redistribute the mended tables to maximum effect. The bits and pieces that were over I added to the growing pile of wreckage in the yard. The kitchen, to the casual glance, was almost back to normal. Gillian was flailing a wet cloth over every surface in sight, jabbering to herself.

I said, 'You've done wonders. Let's take a break.'

She thrust hair out of her eyes. 'We can make our own coffee now, Mr Hunt. I found another kettle in the top cupboard over there. They missed that.'

I expressed joy. Back in the shop, I set about reloading the shelves, most of which had been swept clear by the intruders. A rapping on the window interrupted me. I released the door catch.

'Paul!' Bridget swept through to gaze about her like a duchess inspecting the guest suite after the maids had been in. 'You *poor* boy! Patty and I were aghast when we heard. Phwat on earth were they after, those *dreadful* people? You'd nothing for them to—'

'Does there have to be a reason?'

'Not these days, I suppose. Here comes Patty with the food.'

'The food?' I repeated cautiously.

'We guessed you'd be up to your eyes, so we brought you some lunch. *And* a spot of elbow-grease, if required.' She flexed her arms, bringing down three bags of fruit pastilles from an upper shelf. 'Anything we can do?' she demanded, diving to pick them up and banging her head on the edge of the counter. 'Don't be shy. Put us to work. That's what we're here for.'

I was deeply touched. 'We'll eat first, Bridget. Cold roast duckling—terrific. You're a pearl. Hi, Patty. Thanks for coming along.'

'In time of stress,' he replied solemnly, 'gestures speak louder than words. We insist upon putting in a stint first, don't we, Bridget? We're not going to march straight in and start munching.'

'OK: half an hour, then. Let's see. The tables in the tea-room want polishing and laying with china and so forth . . . what's left of it. The two of you could be making a start on that. Don't press too hard. My carpentry isn't all it could be.'

'Carpentry?'

I explained briefly. Patty looked impressed. 'Joiner and restorer,' he exclaimed, 'in addition to your other talents. That's what I call resource.'

'All I've done is cobble some of it together until I can replace it out of the insurance.'

'You could manufacture some stuff of your own,' he suggested in all seriousness. 'You've a workshop in your garden.'

'Yes, with power laid on. Just find me some tools and an extra six hours a day and I'll get cracking.'

'Ignore him, Paul,' Bridget commanded. 'Come along, Patty, you silly old twerp, let's make a start. We're here to help, not dish out advice on extra-vocational pursuits.'

While I was digging out cleaning materials and bits of surviving crockery for them, I spotted the elfin figure of Lionel Felrose crossing the street. My groan brought Bridget back from the tea-room. 'Phwat's wrong now?'

'Lionel. He's coming to gloat.'

'Send him packing. Don't talk to him, the nasty little worm.'

'Too late. He's here. If you've come to help out,' I told Lionel disingenuously as he presented himself in the doorway, 'we're in need of cutlery. Got any you can spare?'

'Paul, dear old fellow—how could they *do* it to you?' He seemed on the brink of tears. 'All your hard work, just . . . just *dissipated* overnight. How are you feeling? Is there something I can do? Have the police—'

'We're coping. I'm serious about the cutlery. Some of ours seems to have gone missing.'

'I'll see what I can hunt up.' His head made darting movements, like a bird searching for breadcrumbs. 'Your poor shelves. Always so neat and well-stocked, and look at them now.'

'Soon be back to normal. It's just the way things are, these days.'

'Oh dear. You don't think we're due for a *plague*? We've been so lucky up to now. Never any bother.'

'If the worst comes to the worst, we'll organize vigilantes.'

'Paul, you're being frightfully plucky, I do admire you.

As if you hadn't enough on your mind, just now. Friends are a comfort, though, aren't they? Wish I could lend a practical hand myself, but I've nobody to look after the shop.'

'That's all right, Lionel,' hooted Bridget from the connecting door where she had taken refuge. 'You get back to your relics. Think yourself lucky that if any of your junk gets knocked about it should gain enormously in value.'

'It's not a laughing matter, Mrs Sheeney,' he riposted petulantly. 'Any threat to trade in the village is a threat to everyone. Cutlery . . . I'll go and take a look. Excuse me, won't you?'

He flounced out. Bridget gave vent to mirth of such vigour that she struck her head on the door frame. 'I shouldn't bait him, but he's such a little snake. I just want to tread on him.'

'He's not so bad. There's a soft side to his nature.'

'Soft? Spongelike, you mean. He goes about soaking up goodwill and squeezing it out as spite. Ugh!'

'I think you're over-reacting,' I said mildly. With order partly restored, I was starting to feel more charitable. Things might have been worse. The intruders could have set fire to the premises. By mid-afternoon we should be in business again. 'Forget the tables for the moment,' I told Bridget. 'Let's eat now. Afterwards, we can—'

The telephone broke in. 'Hope that's not the police,' I said, 'telling me not to touch anything.' I hoisted the receiver. 'Pantiles. Business as usual. What can I do for you?'

'Mr Paul Hunt?' The voice was male and indifferent. 'Calling on behalf of DCI Duke, sir. He'd like a few more words with you. There's a car on its way.'

CHAPTER 10

The police van had gone from the farmhouse yard. The incident room was now housed in an annexe to the main building, a single-storey attachment evidently used at one time as a dairy. Milk churns were stacked against an end wall. In the centre of the quarry-tiled floor, an oil-fired heater was fighting the chill mustiness of the place. Chief Inspector Duke looked faintly purple. He contemplated me over the heavy bench that had been pressed into use as a worktable.

'Why did you lie to me?'

'I'm not sure what you're getting at.'

'Well then, let me put it to you explicitly. Why did you say you'd never seen Elaine Turner before, when in fact you had?'

'I said I had. The previous day.'

'Stop wasting my time,' he said on a conversational note. 'You know quite well what I mean. You and she were old buddies. Why try to conceal it? You must have known we'd make inquiries.'

I was silent.

He glanced at the tape-recorder, operating busily on the woodwork between us. 'This thing, Mr Hunt, doesn't pick up obstinate expressions, sad to say. The spoken word is what it feeds on. If you want your side of things to be noted, you'd be well advised to come across a little more . . . verbally.' He sat back, chin on knuckles.

'You wouldn't have believed me,' I said after a moment.

'Wouldn't have . . . ?'

'You'd have been even more sceptical than you were about my account of finding her body.'

'Not half as sceptical as we are now. Some initial frankness would have done wonders.'

'What have you found out?'

He studied a typewritten sheet. 'With the aid of our Metropolitan brothers, we've established that you and Miss Turner were on . . . shall we say, exceptionally close terms for a period of a year or so, during which you were a fund manager with the firm of Cashtalk, financial advisers, while she was employed as a sales assistant at a store in the Finchley area. Right so far?'

'Why ask, if you've made inquiries?'

'We like to level the ground as we go along. According to ex-colleagues of yours, you and Elaine Turner had an intense relationship which ended at around the same time as you were dismissed by Cashtalk from your position as acting investments manager with special responsibility for—'

'I left by arrangement.'

Duke fingered his jaw. 'The distinction,' he said dourly, 'is a shade fine to me. Maybe you'd care to enlarge.'

'I don't care to, but I seem to have little choice.' I returned his gaze. 'How much have you dug up of Elaine's history?'

He consulted his notes. 'It would appear to have been somewhat chequered. Putting it bluntly, she was a man-chaser. Before meeting you, she'd already had a number of, hum, dubious liaisons. From our information, she wasn't above conducting a little refined blackmail of more than one of the wedded unfortunates she'd got involved with, threatening to tell all to their wives if they didn't come up with a pay-off . . . a fairly ruthless piece of work, to put it no stronger. You yourself, of course, weren't at risk in that respect. You weren't married.'

'You're sure you want details from me? You seem to have them all at your fingertips.'

'I wouldn't say that. We've got the bare bones. I'd like you to flesh 'em out.'

'Starting from where?'

'The reason for your dismissal . . . your parting from Cashtalk by mutual consent.'

I drew a long, deep breath. 'It's an episode I'd sooner forget. You're right about Elaine: she was poison. I didn't find that out until I'd known her eleven months. I was infatuated. Wanted to marry her, sweep her off: the works. She was that kind of a woman.'

The Chief Inspector nodded, his eyes fixed on me. 'At what point were you . . . enlightened?'

'After I'd defrauded my firm of eighteen thousand quid.'

His eyebrows rose half an inch. 'What made you do that?'

'She did.'

'You mean, wanting to indulge her expensive tastes, you resorted to—'

'No, that isn't what I mean. She was more subtle than that. We'd been going together for a while when up she came with this tale of distress about her mother. According to Elaine, she was desperately ill in a nursing home near Manchester and needed an operation that would cost thousands. The only place she could have it was this Swiss clinic where they were pioneering a new treatment . . . you know the type of thing. It was quite a yarn she spun, and I fell for it.'

'Go on.'

'Feeling as I did about Elaine, I never questioned the story. All that concerned me was that she was in trouble, asking for help.'

'Which you were in a position to give?'

'Like hell I was. The fact that I was advising others on finance had nothing to do with my own situation. I was living up to my income. The sort of money she was talking about was above my orbit. All the same, I was determined she was going to have it.'

'Hence, the eighteen thousand?'

'It wasn't for myself,' I assured him. 'Not directly, that is. It was to make her mother well again, as I thought. I never saw it as misappropriation of funds. At the time, in the state I was in, it seemed perfectly justified. I was sure I'd be able to pay it back.'

'The mental blindness of devotion,' Duke remarked, deadpan. 'So, having bilked the firm of that amount, what did you do? Just hand it over to her?'

'I didn't attach strings, if that's what you mean. I assumed she'd use the money to pack her mother straight off to the Alps. She told me that was what she'd done. I never doubted it.'

'And meanwhile, the cash wasn't missed?'

'It was eventually. It belonged to investors. Should have been in securities, earning our clients an income. When my boss learned what had happened, naturally he was appalled. On two levels.'

Duke's features showed puzzlement. 'How d'you mean?'

'First, he couldn't believe I'd done such a thing. He trusted me.' I passed a hand over my face. 'And the other thing was, the sheer ease I'd done it with. That was the real knockout.'

'The fact remains, though, it *was* discovered . . .'

'Only by a fluke. It showed up because . . . I won't go into all that. The point was, had I been charged and the case had gone to court, Cashtalk would have been mightily embarrassed by what emerged. Their accounting methods and general way of conducting business would have been shown up for what it was: belonging to the Stone Age. They'd have lost credibility and clients.'

'I get it. So they didn't take you to court?'

'It was dealt with on that basis. No charges: no publicity.

The arrangement was that I should leave and the whole affair would be quietly forgotten, for the benefit of all concerned,'

The Chief Inspector sat forward. 'Did they get you to repay the cash?'

'They weren't going to insist on it. In the circumstances, they were willing to swallow hard and take the loss. But I couldn't have quit with that on my conscience. My father, bless him, came across with an interest-free loan, and I reimbursed them with that.'

Duke eyed me pensively. 'How about your subsequent relationship with Miss Turner?'

I felt my mouth twitch. 'The moment I was out of a job, she grafted on to someone else. I'd served my purpose.'

'The sick mother, I take it, never existed?'

'She had a mother, but she was as strong as an ox, running some nightclub in Liverpool. I found that out, too late, from other sources.'

Duke sat ruminating. 'So there you were, disillusioned, flat broke, out of a career . . . I'm starting to see why you opted for the quiet life in a village teashop. Why here, in particular?'

'A friend of mine who'd moved down here chanced to mention that the Pantiles had become vacant, and half-jokingly suggested I might take it on. He knew I was looking for something.'

'What did you do for capital?'

'Raised a bank mortgage. Cashtalk kept their word not to damage my credit rating. I aim to make a go of it. My prime objective is to repay that loan to my father within three years.'

'What are your chances?'

'Up until lately, I thought they were reasonable. Trade has been picking up and I've forged links with the locals. By and large, they're a good bunch. Then this happens.'

Duke made an absent-minded adjustment to the tape-recorder. 'Must have come as a nasty shock when you first discovered that Miss Turner had added herself to the electoral roll. You still insist that you weren't aware of her identity until you called here with a couple of messages?'

'Nobody was.'

'No doubt you wondered why the devil she'd turned up here like a bad penny. Maybe you assumed she was hounding you or something. What explanation did she give?'

'Elaine wasn't into explanations.'

Duke made a sound in his throat that could have denoted either assent, cynicism or hilarity. 'She did refer vaguely,' I added, 'to being scared of someone: having to hide out while the heat subsided. Something of that nature.'

'Really?'

'I'm not making this up,' I snarled. 'That's why she wanted me to bring supplies. She wanted to avoid venturing out herself.'

'Might have helped if you'd told me all this before.'

'Well, you know how it is. Us civilian mortals, we do tend to stampede a bit under pressure. By the time we've come to terms—'

'All right, simmer down.' He sat appraising me. 'If she was still toxic to you,' he resumed presently, 'why did you agree to bring her the provisions? I'd have thought you'd have left her to stew in her own juice.'

'It was a spot of business. I need all I can get.'

'She was going to pay you?'

'Of course.'

'And you were quite happy about that?' he said sardonically.

'If she hadn't paid up, cash on delivery, I wouldn't have left the stuff.'

Duke reflected. 'Seems to me it would have been more

natural for you to run a mile at the sight of her, sooner than
risk getting involved again. Unless, that is . . .'

'Unless what?'

'You still held a torch for her.'

'With that . . . creature?'

'OK, so you didn't. In which case, I say again, why get
re-embroiled at all? Unless there was an element of coercion
about it.'

I gave him a straight look. 'Even assuming that Elaine
knew what I'd done at Cashtalk—and I never told her in
detail—there was nothing she could have revealed to them
that they didn't already know.'

'Maybe; but I wasn't necessarily thinking in terms of
what she might have told Cashtalk. Closer to home could
have been more effective, don't you think?'

'Now what are you implying?'

'Look at it from an objective point of view. Here's a young
fellow like yourself, saddled with debt, trying desperately to
build up a business in a neighbourhood where tongues start
wagging if a duck crosses the road . . . when along comes
somebody who, if she'd a mind to, could easily blight your
prospects by the simple expedient of dropping a word here,
a hint there: you know the sort of thing. Heard about that
Paul Hunt, up at the Pantiles? Bit of a murky past, they
tell me. Some financial jiggery-pokery. Thousands
involved. Catch me setting foot in that shop of his again.
Fellow could rook you as soon as blink.' Duke sat back with
folded arms, assessing my reaction.

The fact that he was horribly close to the mark did nothing for my composure. 'I've never heard such tosh.'

He was unruffled. 'As an ex-financier, you must surely
be aware of what a whispering campaign can do to an
individual's credibility. You're in no position to ride a
slump in your trade. To say nothing of the respect and
friendship you've accumulated in and around the village,

which you evidently value. You've a status to protect. If Elaine Turner had even insinuated—'

Rising from my chair, I walked over to the milk churns and gave one of them a resounding kick. The police sergeant who was stationed at the door watched me impassively. Chief Inspector Duke didn't bother to turn round.

'If I'm to be swayed,' he instructed the opposite wall, 'it's going to take logical counter-argument, not physical assaults on farming equipment.'

I swivelled round. 'The reverse could equally be true. If I were to gain a reputation as something of a lad, the Pantiles might acquire a cachet of its own. I could have experienced an upsurge of custom, rather than the reverse.'

'Intriguing point. But maybe you preferred not to put it to the test. A silenced Elaine Turner could pose no threat, one way or the other.'

'You're talking through your hat.'

'Comes out muffled, does it? I'm having the same problem with you. It's all woolly, Mr Hunt, all thick-textured and hard on the ears. What I need is something distinct, that I can hear and understand.'

I returned to my seat. 'I don't see what more I can give. You've now got the entire background. There isn't any more.'

'Which brings us to the nub of the matter. Were you, or were you not, set upon by the killer of Elaine Turner as he made his escape? Or is it a story you've concocted in an attempt to get yourself off the hook?'

I sat dredging my resources for a body-punch, one that would take the wind out of him. Inspiration fluttered down. 'You've no evidence,' I said triumphantly. 'The reason you're trying to wear me down like this is that you can't prove I did it.'

Rising serenely in his turn, Duke collected something from a nearby cabinet, returning to plant the item with a

certain meticulous finality on the bench, two feet from my
nose. I looked up at him.

'Showing me the murder weapon again is hardly going
to tip me over the edge.'

'What would you say if I told you that your fingerprints
were on it?'

'I'd ask how you could possibly know. You don't have
my prints.'

His smile held a touch of weariness. 'We don't? There's
a dozen places we could have got them from. Your motor
vehicle, your shop premises, the chair-back you were grasp-
ing the last time I interviewed you . . . In actual fact, a
glazed chinaware surface takes some beating, and you were
provided, if you recall, with a cup of coffee on a previous
occasion.'

'What a pointless subterfuge,' I scoffed. 'Why didn't you
just ask me for them?'

'I could have. But that would have sounded more alarms,
set you dreaming up further alibis. Now, I'd like a straight
answer. If you didn't give Elaine Turner this clock, and if
you didn't grab it up for some purpose within the past few
days, how did your prints get on the damn thing?'

'If it's true that they are, then the answer's obvious.
Having knocked me cold, the killer wiped the clock clean,
then pressed it into my hand as I lay there.'

'Before stowing it in the back of your Land-Rover,
returning to his own car and driving off?'

'Seems obvious.'

The Chief Inspector gazed into space. 'Active little fellow, wasn't he, in the few moments he must have had
between crime and escape?'

'Active? Of course he was active. In a situation like that,
you don't sit around if you've any sense.' I sat glowering
at him. 'For that matter, how do we know he only had a

few moments? I could have been out for anything up to half
an hour.'

Duke made no comment. It seemed to me he looked a
little less sure of himself. I swam in on the tide. 'There's
nothing whatever in the facts you've given me that can't be
accounted for in support of what I've said. Deny that if you
can.'

His mouth twitched. 'You're perfectly right, of course.
All the facts can be accounted for. On your terms: and
equally on ours. Unless and until we trace this other man,
we shan't know for certain, shall we?'

CHAPTER 11

Dusk was assembling as I slammed the kitchen door of the
cottage and snapped on the light. I was in a mood appropriate to the clashing of locks and the thumbing of switches.
The more noise it made, the better I liked it at the moment.
Striding through to the telephone, I tried the Pantiles
number. Unremarkably, there was no reply. I called
Timbers.

Patty answered. 'Yes, my boy. We left around three.
Young Gillian was still at it. She's a brick, that girl. How
did you get on with the Inspector?'

'*Chief* Inspector,' I growled. 'He's touchy about the pre-
fix. How did I get on? I suggest you ask him. He wasn't
letting me in on the secret.'

'Not charged you yet, then?'

'It's about all he hasn't done.'

'Never mind, my boy. It'll blow over. While I remember:
Bridget says you're to come to lunch again next Wednesday.'

'Assuming I'm still at large. Thanks, Patty. And double

thanks for what you did today, the pair of you. I shan't forget. Did Gillian manage to open up, finally?'

'She was talking about it,' Patty said vaguely. 'You'll learn tomorrow, no doubt. By the by, Paul, something else I meant to mention. I was passing your place an hour or two ago—scouting for Reggie, as a matter of fact—when I noticed your cover.'

'My what?'

'The manhole thing at the foot of your bank, in the side lane. On the way down to the spinney, you know.'

'Yes. What about it?'

'That tub you keep on it, with the hanging plants— somebody seems to have been meddling with it. It was half on the metal and half on the grass, a bit lopsided. I put it straight for you.'

I ground my teeth. 'That'll be Myrtle. Or Don. Or a combined op. They'll have been taking a sneaky look at the sewage flow from a different angle. They're obsessed. Thanks again, Patty. I'll tackle them about it.'

'They didn't cause any damage . . .'

'Considerate of them. But if they must go around lifting inspection covers, they might at least put 'em back as they found them. All they can think of is their damn cesspool.'

'Don's an obliging chap, in some ways,' Patty said diplomatically. 'He's useful with his hands. If you asked him, he'd probably be glad to bring his power tools along to that workshop of yours and help you restore a bit more of the furniture from the Pantiles. He'd make a decent—'

'I'm sure he would,' I said wearily. 'On the other hand, it'll be quicker and easier to order a job lot from Jepson's out of the insurance money, if I get it . . . if I'm around to receive it. See you Wednesday, I hope. Love to Bridget.' I hung up before he could think of something else to tell me, and returned to the kitchen.

Resentment against Myrtle and Don Jones and their preoccupation with domestic sludge helped to take my mind off the Chief Inspector, though not greatly. Trying to open a can of corned beef, I sliced my thumb and was searching the cottage for a plaster when the telephone shrilled. I ran downstairs to lift the receiver, distributing blood generously over the instrument. 'Yes?'

'This is Angela Peterson.'

'Yes?'

'Did you get my message?'

'Message?'

'Apparently you didn't. I rang the shop this afternoon, but you weren't there. The girl said she'd let you know I wanted to get in touch with you.'

'I've not spoken to Gill since lunch-time. I've only just got home.' To avoid explanations I added hurriedly, 'How can I help you?'

'I'm interested in one of Sandra Millett's paintings.'

'Oh yes?'

'The one of Bobdean Manor. I understand it was damaged by intruders last night.'

'I'm afraid so. Did you want to buy it?'

'I'd like to look at it. Was it badly affected?'

'It's in halves.'

'Oh. Well, I might still be interested. If the two parts aren't actually defaced . . .'

'I've got them here in the Land-Rover. I was going to run them along to Sandra in case she wants to do a repair job. She'd be glad to show it to you, I'm sure, at her studio.'

'But not until tomorrow, presumably?'

'Why, is it urgent?'

'It is a little. Look, say if it's inconvenient, but . . . Could I possibly call along this evening?'

'Here?'

'Yes, at your cottage. I don't want to interrupt your evening, but it's difficult for me to get away from the school during the day and, as I said, I would like to see it as soon as possible.'

I swallowed hard. 'Pop along by all means. I'll have the bits ready for you.'

Snatching a few bites of the corned beef and a spoonful of baked beans, I considered this sudden enthusiasm for Sandra's work on the part of the schoolteacher. Why Bobdean Manor, specifically? It was a nineteenth-century structure of routine appeal, situated on the fringe of a nearby hamlet of the same name and formerly owned, Roger Ashby had told me, by an Anglophile American who had dwelt there for a decade or more before being obliged to return to California to take command of the family hypermarket business. With conversion to other uses in mind, speculators were rumoured to have cast glances in the direction of the building, but nothing had yet transpired. Ashby himself had spoken mysteriously of his plans for the place. Like many of his projects, however, it seemed to have remained at the embryo stage. I frequently gained the impression that he derived more enjoyment from talking about property deals than pursuing them to a conclusion.

Maybe, I thought, Angela was a student of early Victorian architecture, writing a thesis on the topic which had to be completed within the next twenty-four hours. It seemed improbable, and in any event she was a pest; I didn't feel up to coping with her. Only the chance of making a sale on Sandra's behalf had persuaded me to agree to her visit. An hour later, when her footsteps approached along the path, my mood had worsened. I met her at the kitchen door with a straight face.

'Hi. Step right in. I've spread the halves on the living-room table so that you can get an idea.' Basic courtesy forced me to add, 'Can I take your . . . coat?'

'I'll keep it on, thanks.' The garment in question was a thigh-length affair of zips, buckles and pegs, more in the

nature of makeshift light armour than rustic attire. It gave
her the appearance of being heavily encased but at the same
time deprived of contact with the material, as though any
rotatory movement on her part would have left the jacket
stationary and suspended. There was a faint pink flush to
her cheeks. 'I'm in a bit of a rush. Through here?'

'A quick drink? I've got—'

'Nothing for me, thanks.' From a short distance she surveyed the remains of Sandra's picture. 'It's not too bad,'
she commented.

'The painting? Or the damage?'

'Oh, I like the picture. She's captured the place well.'

'She goes into very painstaking detail.'

'Is all her work like this?'

'Better, in my opinion. Though I know nothing about
art. What do you think? Is it repairable?'

Eyeing the pieces, she said nothing. I coughed. 'I'm sure
Sandra wouldn't expect full price for the thing as it stands.
Undamaged, it was forty quid.'

'If I offered you twenty?'

I reached a quick decision. 'Sounds fair.'

'Sandra wouldn't object?'

'She's given me *carte blanche* to negotiate.'

'Fine,' Angela said briskly. 'I'll write you a cheque.'

Extracting pen and book from her bag, she did so in
athletic fashion, with a wealth of flourishes and elongated
hyphenry. Ripping off the sheet, she held it out. 'I might
be interested in some of her other work, in due course.'

'Great. I'll tell her.'

Furling the halves carefully, Angela slid the resulting
canister under her arm. I said, 'Let me find you a carrier.'

'Don't bother.'

'You might drop it in the mud.' I went out to the kitchen
for a plastic bag from the supermarket. When I turned from
the drawer she was almost at my elbow, conducting an

inscrutable examination of the kitchen layout. I was forcibly reminded of how small she was. The top of her hair just cleared the level of my shoulder. A whiff of scent hung in the air. Taking the scroll from her, I enfolded it in polythene. 'Sure you won't stay for that drink?'

'Thank you, I won't. I've another appointment.' She moved towards the outer door.

Perversely, I felt a little nettled. Five minutes ago I had wanted to be rid of her. A quick image of her in the lounge bar of the Stag the previous evening, absorbed in Ashby's conversation, prompted my next, incautious remark. 'So, you're not in need of a hair of the dog?'

'I beg your pardon?'

'My head was spinning when I left the pub last night. You were still there, I noticed.'

'Perhaps you should space out the double whiskies,' she said coolly, opening the door.

'Easier said than done, in convivial company. Have a good time?'

'It was quite pleasant. I was talking to Mr Ashby.'

'So I noticed.'

'Some reason I shouldn't?'

'No. No. His wife wasn't with him?'

'I don't know. I imagine not.'

'You did realize he's married?'

One of her feet had reached the cement outside. She brought it back inside the kitchen. Her gaze slanted up into my face in such a way that it seemed to be slanting down.

'When I need information, Mr Hunt, on the marital status of the local population, I'll ask for it. Though probably not from you. Thank you for selling me the painting. Good night.'

Her heels clacked away to the gate, which opened and closed with some force. I hit my head lightly, several times, against the doorframe. Guerrilla warfare between the two of us seemed predestined, like the hostility between tribes. Every dialogue we had took a header into the nearest ditch. The suspicion that it was chiefly my fault was not helpful to my self-esteem, but now that she had gone there was nothing to be done, and in any case I had other things to think about.

I sat in the living-room with a glass of diluted brandy in my fist and thought about them.

The broad vowels of the chief inspector lost no time in gaining the upper hand, marching in line astern through the echoing canyons of my mind. 'You can go, Mr Hunt . . . for the moment. But I'll want to talk to you again. You've at last told me a fair bit: question is, how much else is there for you to come clean about? I just wonder, that's all . . .'

The floor was jumping under my feet.

I came out of a restless dream with a sensation of being tossed around. The chair springs seemed to be vibrating and twanging beneath me. Thrusting myself clear, I retreated to the kitchen, shut the door on the shuddering noise that had invaded the adjoining room, stood gripping the back of a chair while I debated what to do. The time was a little after ten. Grabbing my jacket from its hook, I put it on and left the cottage.

Passing Timbers, I slowed the Land-Rover while I looked across for signs of life. There was no trace of light in any window; the Sheeneys were either out or in bed. I accelerated away, listening to a radio broadcast of what sounded like a Restoration comedy. It was therapeutic to hear voices of any kind. They accompanied me as far as the village main street, where I switched the radio off and slackened pace again to a crawl, mentally alert once more, but indecisive. To my right, the windows of the Pantiles cast a glow across the footway. Faithful to my instructions, Gillian had left lights blazing in a bid to discourage marauders. My right foot groped for the brake, hesitated, returned to the throttle. I was not in an investigative frame of mind.

Continuing to the end of the shopping area, I pulled up opposite a terrace of tile-hung dwellings which stood back from the street to form a courtyard. Behind the curtains of one of the ground-floor windows, radiance was visible. Leaving the Land-Rover at the kerbside, I crossed the cobbled approach to the relevant front door and gave it a discreet rapping with the knocker.

It was opened almost immediately, fully, unrestricted by a chain. Sandra peeped out, shielding her eyes against a street light. 'Why, Mr Hunt! What a surprise.'

'If I've called at a bad time . . .'

'Gosh, no. John wasn't sleepy, so we're watching the late film. Come along in.'

'I'll be interrupting.'

'Yes, and thank goodness for that. The film's an utter dud. John, it's Mr . . . It's Paul Hunt from the Pantiles. The teashop—you know.'

She blanked out the screen while her brother winched his right hand across at waist level to receive mine. 'Sandra's told me about you,' he volunteered, gasping slightly. 'I gather she's suckered you into . . . turning your place into . . . an art gallery.'

'That's what I'm here about.'

He and his sister exchanged comic faces. 'Didn't I say he'd rebel? He's had enough.'

Sandra looked troubled. 'We heard about your break-in. Was it awfully bad?'

'It was untidy. And I'm sorry to say—'

'They wrecked my pictures? I was afraid of that. I did think of calling in this afternoon to ask, but I guessed you'd enough on your plate, clearing up the mess. Any way I can help?'

'We're practically back to normal, thanks. About your paintings: it's not as bad as you think. Three of them were untouched. The fourth was ripped in half, but I think it's repairable.'

'There you go!' John Millett beamed at his sister. He had very dark hair which tumbled over one eye, giving him a lopsided appearance that was accentuated by his posture in the wheelchair, heeling to starboard so that his right elbow took the weight of the upper half of his body. His lower limbs were covered by a rug. Although I knew him to be several years older than Sandra, he looked younger; notwithstanding the shortness of breath, there was a marked element of boyishness about him. 'Said you were . . . panicking without cause, didn't I?'

'When did you say that?' She flicked his quiff with the back of a hand. 'I don't remember. Three of them survived, then? That's a relief. I was gearing myself up to dash off a few quickies to make up the numbers. But perhaps you'd . . .' She eyed me doubtfully. 'If you'd sooner not have the responsibility of them any more, you've only got to say.'

'There's good news, actually. I've just sold the two bits.'

'You've done what?'

'Sold the one they tore apart: the Bobdean Manor. Half-price, I'm afraid, but fair's fair. The buyer seemed very taken with it.'

'Who is it? Anyone we know?'

'Angela Peterson, the schoolteacher.'

'Oh! Goodness. She struck me as very blue-stocking when I met her at the Flower Show. How marvellous. I wonder why she chose that one?'

'She seemed rather intent on having it. Came all the way over to my place this evening to clinch the deal.'

John puffed. 'Maybe she has some . . . personal interest in the Manor.'

'Maybe she appreciates good art,' retorted Sandra. 'I've always had a soft spot for that one, myself. Does she want me to patch it up for her?'

'I got the impression she might do it herself. You could ask her.'

'In a way, I'd sooner she left it to me. Not that I don't appreciate her buying it. My first sale! We should drink to this. Paul? What'll you have?'

'There's only medium sherry,' remarked her brother.

'It's polite to ask. He might fancy lemon barley water.'

'Funnily enough,' I told her, 'that's exactly what would go down nicely. I seem to have had a surfeit of alcohol just lately. Must keep a clear head. I suspect I'm going to need it. Here.' Taking her hand, I turned it palm uppermost and placed a quartet of five-pound notes into position. She stared down at them.

'What's this?'

'In full and prompt settlement.'

'Are you sure? I really don't mind waiting.'

'No need. I've Angela's cheque in my wallet.'

'But what about your commission?'

'To mark your first triumph, I hereby waive my nominal ten per cent. And I hope it's merely the first of many.' I hesitated. 'Angela did indicate that she might be interested in others from you.'

'Gosh.' Sandra looked at her brother with shining eyes. 'I'd better start producing a few.'

'Working on something now?'

'You bet.' Diffidently she edged towards the door. 'Time for a quick look?'

'Sure.'

On the way upstairs she said, 'Nice of you to pop over so quickly to break the news. With all your other problems.'

'Not entirely an unselfish act,' I admitted. 'I wanted to talk to someone.'

Pausing on the uncarpeted landing, lit by a low-power bulb fixed to a beam, she turned to look at me. 'You mean you were . . . I mean . . .'

'Lonesome? Not as a rule. But I'm having some trouble at the cottage. Noises. This evening they were so bad, I just wanted to get out. So here I am.'

I awaited her next question with some confidence. It arrived on cue. 'What sort of noises?'

I described them briefly. She frowned. 'We get strange little poppings and hiccups all the time. It's these old places, I expect. Things expand during the day, then contract at night, and then you get—'

'I'm sure you're right,' I agreed, dismissing the topic. 'Show me this latest masterwork of yours.'

'I'm barely half way through it,' she said defensively, opening a door and switching on lights. 'Besides which, you need daylight to see it properly. You'll have to make allowances.'

The room was attic-style, large and chaotic. Finished canvases were stacked against one wall; framing materials against another, which also accommodated a trestle table bearing tubes of paint, brushes and colour-streaked cloths. Dead-centre of the room stood an easel, beneath a skylight. Sandra led me round to face it.

'Looks familiar,' I said after a moment.

Her hand went to her mouth. 'I was forgetting . . . I'm sorry, I should have warned you. How could I be so thoughtless? I wasn't—'

'Relax. The sight of it gave me a jolt, that's all. You're working from photos, as usual?'

'Yes. In fact, I took them on the very morning you went along and . . .' She tripped over the words.

'Stumbled on a corpse,' I said helpfully.

Sandra nodded. 'It occurred to me later, she could have

been . . . lying there the whole time I was taking shots from outside.'

'She probably . . .' I turned to stare at her. 'Hey, that's a thought. You didn't happen to see anyone while you were there? On the premises, or in the neighbourhood?'

'If I had, I'd have reported it. As far as I could tell, there wasn't a soul about.'

I restored my attention to her faithful portrayal of Prior's Farm, viewed from the rear across a paddock. 'Did you knock first?' I asked presently.

'I'd heard she never answered the door. There didn't seem any harm in going round the back way—there's a secondary track, you know, down from the lane further on—and taking some shots from there without disturbing anybody.' Sandra gave me a sidelong glance. 'Do you think that was a sneaky thing to do?'

'There's no law I know of that bans outside photography, as long as you don't cause damage. Coming along nicely, isn't it? Pleased with it?'

She pulled a face. 'I'm never pleased with *anything*.'

'Angela wouldn't agree with you.'

'Pleasing other people is a different matter.' She led the way out of the studio and downstairs again. 'Paul thinks I'm a genius,' she announced. 'Well, a half-way competent draughtswoman, anyhow. And he's been plagued by noises in his cottage, John. Any suggestions?'

I said, 'You mustn't concern yourselves with—'

'But John might have some ideas. He's brilliant, actually. Just you try him.'

Her brother slipped me a whimsical glance. 'Easily impressed, my kid sister. What's the trouble? Mice in the loft?'

By now word-perfect, I gave him a concise recitation. Having listened attentively, he spent a few moments in thought. 'Doesn't sound like rodents . . .'

'I've been putting poison down, but there's no sign of it being taken. Besides, it's just not that sort of noise. One of the local farmhands suggests it might be an electrical fault. The immersion heater, perhaps. He's supposed to be having a look at it some time.'

Sandra's brother meditated. 'He could have something. Water and electricity can be a funny combination. Might easily lead to all manner of wails and screams.'

'But the hot water cylinder's upstairs,' I objected. 'Why would the sound seem to come from under the living-room floor?'

'Might depend on your wiring. If it ran beneath the floorboards . . . I'm not sure. It would need a proper inspection.'

'I expect I'll end up having the whole place taken apart,' I said gloomily.

'There again, your plumbing might be to blame. Are you on main drainage?'

I uttered a cavernous groan. 'If Parsons Lane were on main drainage, you would see before you a happy man. As it is, my cess tank has the misfortune to be situated in my neighbours' garden. They're paranoiac about it.'

'To get to the tank, would the pipes from your bathroom have to run under the living-room?'

'It's certainly in a more or less direct line. But there seem to be inspection chambers all over the place. There's one, for instance, to the right of the cottage, the opposite side from my neighbours. I can't get the hang of the system.'

'Might there be some old ducting that meanders under your place, giving access to some nocturnal creature?'

'Like an African elephant?' I suggested. 'No, I'm not dismissing the idea. It could be something of that kind, although if so, the wildlife around here must need tranquillizers. Thanks, John. You've given me one or two things to think about. Now I must be off. Sorry to barge in like that. Put it down to desperation.'

'Call in any time,' urged Sandra. 'We love to see people.'

'Even murder suspects?'

'I wouldn't worry about that. I'm sure the police can't really imagine you'd anything to do with it.'

On the way back, I halted the Land-Rover outside the Pantiles.

Through the lighted windows, I could see that Gillian had left everything immaculate. Inside the shop, the shelves were fully restocked and fresh price tags had replaced those that had been annihilated; the tea-room, with its fewer tables, looked less disorderly than it had before the raid. I made a mental note to take Gillian and the Sheeneys for a celebratory lunch somewhere when the dust had settled. Such a gesture would have the dual advantage of repaying their loyalty and avoiding further exposure to Bridget's charred roast duckling. The Tudor Barn Restaurant, maybe, in Brampton Valley. I had been meaning to try it for some time. Engaging gear, I was about to move off when I noticed that there was light, too, on the other side of the street. It came from Lionel Felrose's showroom.

Twenty minutes before midnight seemed an unusual hour for him to be working. A movement at the back of the showroom caught my eye. On the basis of trader solidarity, I opened the door of the Land-Rover stealthily and crossed the road to take an unobtrusive but closer look.

Nothing of a violent nature seemed to be happening inside. From the lee of a high-backed chair on display in the window, I could make out two figures at the rear of the premises. The one facing me was Lionel himself; he was flapping his arms and giving the floor an occasional light stamp with his left foot, as he was prone to do when ani-mated about something. The other man had his back to me. As I watched, Lionel took something from his breast pocket and passed it over. After that they shook hands.

Armed thugs, I reasoned, were not noted for observing the civilities. A man of Lionel's propensities doubtless had some dubious acquaintances; whatever was being transacted, in any case, was no business of mine. Returning quietly to the Land-Rover, I drove off.

All the way home, I tried without success to pin an identity upon the second man. His back had remained towards me throughout, and the lighting had been patchy; nevertheless, something about the shape of him and his stance had been oddly familiar.

CHAPTER 12

Five minutes after opening time the next morning, Roger Ashby tramped into the shop, paused and looked around. 'Somebody spreading false rumours? I understood you'd been taken apart.'

'So we was,' affirmed Gillian on her way to the kitchen. 'We put it together again.'

'What you now see,' I told him, 'is the outcome of resilience and tenacity . . . especially on the part of this young lady here. Thanks for your ready assistance, by the way.'

'I was out of the area,' he explained. 'Never heard about it until Sal told me, late last night. Otherwise, of course, I'd have been here like a shot, pulling my weight.'

'Of course.'

'Any chance of coffee and a doughnut? It's a bit early . . .'

'There's a few over from yesterday, Mr Ashby. I can crisp 'em up for you.'

'That'll do.' He beckoned me through to the tea-room.

'You know,' he observed, taking up a position from which he could examine the remaining three of Sandra's pictures, 'I've been having second thoughts about this output of your protégée. Maybe I was a bit hasty in my judgement. What she does, she does with a certain flair.'

'Changed your mind about having one?'

'Don't jostle me. I still think they err somewhat on the photographic side. Let me think about it.'

'Don't agonise too long,' I advised him. 'An acquaintance of yours has snapped one up already. And she may be back for more.'

'Who's this?'

'Angela, our schoolmarm. She came up with the cash yesterday.'

Ashby looked amused. 'I might have guessed. We were chatting in the Stag the other night—'

'So I noticed.'

'On matters artistic,' he said with a wink, 'as well as scholastic. Got a good head on her, that girl.'

'It certainly seemed to appeal to you.'

'Don't get the wrong idea, old son. I'd never dream of doing anything to hurt Sal. My interest was entirely academic, I can assure you. It's just that I happened to mention young Sandra's work—we were discussing art in general—and I asked Angela whether she'd been in here to see it.'

'She hadn't.'

'So I understand. Anyway, when I said the view of Bobdean Manor struck me as the best of the bunch, I spotted a gleam in Angela's eye. She started asking questions about it. I got the distinct impression she was interested, though I never imagined she'd be so fast on the draw . . . so to speak. Stumped up the asking price, did she?'

'No. It was damaged in the raid, so she got it half price.' I sat opposite him at the window table. 'Can't say I thought it was Sandra's very best, myself. I prefer her latest.'

'Oh? What's that?'

'A rear view of that house of ill-fame, Prior's Farm.'

Ashby's explosion of mirth startled Gillian as she came in, causing her to throw a plateful of hot doughnuts into a recess. After the catastrophe had been dealt with and Gillian placated, she returned to the kitchen for replacements while I reclaimed my chair to fix him with a look. 'What's so funny?'

'Didn't you see the way that doughnut attached itself to the ornamental plate . . .'

'I mean, about Prior's Farm?'

'Oh, that. Well, of all the subjects. For Heaven's sake!'

'She wasn't to know, when she picked on it. Now that she's taken the photographs, I suppose she didn't like to waste them.'

'When did she take them?'

'Believe it or not, the very morning of the murder.'

'No kidding? Did she see anything?'

'Apparently not. She must have left before it happened. Come to think of it, I passed her along the lane as I was making for the place.'

'Always works from photos, does she?'

'Yes. She can't leave her brother for too long.'

'Well, on reflection, she may have chosen well this time. An authentic painting of Prior's Farm could appeal to an art-loving criminologist with a quid or two to spare.' Ashby regarded me thoughtfully. 'Cops still putting you through the hoop?'

'The DCI had another go at me yesterday. Seems convinced that I might have wanted Elaine out of the way, for some reason.'

'But you'd finished with her some while ago, you told me.'

'Quite.' I had no wish to go into further detail, even for

the benefit of Ashby, who had known of our liaison at the
time. While taking a tolerant view of mortal weaknesses,
he was scarcely the person to entrust with information that
one wanted kept strictly to oneself. He was too fond of a
good dialogue, especially with a bar counter to lean on.
'Maybe Duke will lay off,' I added hopefully, 'when they
finally trace this other guy.'

'Which other guy?'

'The one who thumped me. The killer.'

'Do they have any leads?'

'Search me.' I stood up. 'Duke did let slip that they'd
found tyre marks in the mud at the back of the farmhouse,
out of sight from the yard. Marks that didn't tally with the
treads on my Land-Rover, nor Elaine's Fiat. If they could
somehow identify that vehicle and locate its owner . . . Slim
chance, but so far it's all they've got.'

'Did he sound hopeful?'

'DCI Duke,' I said witheringly, 'is hardly the type to
exude optimism. From where I'm standing, he'd much
sooner do a quick, tidy job of arresting me. Here comes
your back-up nourishment; strapped to the dish, I guess,
with rubber bands. I must get back to the shop.'

'Chin up, old son. They can't question you indefinitely.'

As if to stress the fallaciousness of this argument, the call
from the Chief Inspector came through a few minutes later.
'Spare us a few more moments of your time, Mr Hunt? I'm
sending a car.'

'As I've already told you,' I said, 'I did borrow a Fiesta for
a day while my Land-Rover was out of action. That's the
only other vehicle I used to the farm. But I certainly never
took it round to the back.'

Duke shook his head. 'We've eliminated the Fiesta, in
any case. The tyres don't belong to that.'

'What sort of car was likely to have them?'

He shrugged. 'Be useful to know, wouldn't it? Medium size, middle-range type, at a guess. We're still trying to establish an exact pattern so that we can get a line on the make.'

'How do we know,' I demanded, 'when those marks were made? They could have been there for weeks.'

'Unlikely. We'd had a long, dry spell up to a few days ago. That mud is of recent manufacture.'

'Well, I can't think of any other . . . Have you tried the Rector?'

'What's he got to do with it?'

'Nothing, I should hope. But his wife had called at the farm at least a couple of times, he told me. She was hoping to add Elaine's scalp to the Ladies' Circle.'

'Might she have taken her car to the back?'

'Yes, because she tried the doors of the Fiat.'

'What make of car does she run?'

'I've no idea. Could be worth checking.'

Duke made a languid note. 'Any other bright suggestions?'

'If you don't like my contribution, what did you get me here for?'

'I never said I didn't like it. One keeps an open mind. It has to be said, Mr Hunt: overall, I'm not wild about your version of events. Which doesn't mean I intend to neglect other avenues of inquiry. For example . . .'

Reaching into a cabinet drawer, he produced a folder. 'We've probed a bit deeper,' he went on, squinting at its contents, 'into Elaine's background and come up with a fairly seamy lot of this and that. She seems to have rubbed shoulders for years with a highly questionable bunch. Among her closer associates during the past couple of years was . . .' He allowed a brief pause for effect. 'None other than Willy Cashanti.'

'The casino owner?'

'The *crooked* casino operator,' he corrected me, 'with suspected drug-running and illegal immigrant links. Ever run
across him?'

'What kind of company do you imagine I keep?'

'You kept Elaine's.'

'That was different. I knew nothing about her at first.
Now that I'm older and wiser, I can see that she might
have chummed up with anybody. In fact, Cashanti is just
the sort of character she'd have made a beeline for.'

'How do you know?'

I kept my fury in check. 'I know nothing of him personally, if that's what you're implying. Cashanti and the Mafia
are a bit out of my league, wouldn't you say?'

'But not out of Elaine's?'

'Probably not. She could be utterly ruthless in trying to
feather her nest.'

'Same goes for Cashanti. Do you think her involvement
with him might have had something to do with her use of
Prior's Farm as a bolthole? Her fear of being tracked down?'

'Why ask me? I've told you all I know on that score.
From the hints she let drop, I gathered she was in hiding:
somebody, for some reason, was after her. But she never
went into detail.'

Duke tilted his head to gaze at the ceiling. 'Maybe she'd
got to hear of things. Potentially incriminating data. Stuff
that Cashanti was anxious to keep . . . confidential.'

'If she had, I can understand his consternation. Knowing
Elaine, she'd have used it to her own advantage like a shot.
It's a strong possibility, isn't it, Chief Inspector?' I was
starting to get excited. 'Say she'd got hold of some delicate
information and was trying to hold it over him. Say
Cashanti reacted more dangerously than she'd expected,
as a result of which she took fright and—'

'That's an awful lot of surmise. Which is more than can
be said, Mr Hunt, regarding your own part in this affair.

In your case, there exists a considerable body of evidence: concrete as well as circumstantial. We don't owe you any favours. I'd be perfectly within my rights to level charges against you right this minute, never mind about looking into these vague alternatives you keep on about.'

'You're the one,' I said mildly, 'who brought up the name of Cashanti.'

'I know. It's the only reason I'm still listening to you.'

'Too kind,' I said ironically. 'If I'm allowed one more suggestion: why don't you get your team to take a look at any vehicles owned by Cashanti and his associates? That might get you somewhere.'

Duke studied me kindly. 'If Cashanti had wanted Elaine disposed of, you surely don't think he'd have sent a minion out in his own Metro to do the job? Any car used in the operation would have been untraceable. Furthermore—'

'OK. I'm convinced.'

'I'm not dismissing the idea out of hand. Manipulation of drugs and immigrants adds up to serious money. If she knew things, Elaine might well have been in fear of her life. Which could account for her readiness to lie for weeks at a stretch in what can hardly be described—' Duke's gaze strayed disapprovingly to the furthermost corners of the dairy—'as the last word in rural residential splendour. You're with me there, I take it, Mr Burnshaw?'

I blinked across the table at him. 'What's that you called me?'

'The name means nothing to you?'

'Burnshaw? Should it?'

'It's the one—almost certainly false—given by the person who rented this slum on Elaine's behalf.'

'You don't say? Well, it wasn't me.'

He put a good face on it. 'Once more, I've only your word to go on. Nobody around here seems to have clapped eyes on this Burnshaw. According to the letting agent, it was all done by telephone and correspondence. So it could have been anyone.'

'Hard luck on you.'

'Harder still on you.'

'If it's misfortune we're talking about, count me in as an expert. Anything more you want me for, Chief Inspector? I do have a teashop to run.'

'Oh yes. How are the premises now, by the way? Got 'em roughly back into shape?'

'With the aid of some good friends,' I said significantly. 'No thanks to anybody else.'

At the top of the track I turned the Land-Rover left along the lane, away from the village.

Within a quarter of a mile I saw the entrance to the secondary track that Sandra had spoken of. Overgrown and rutted, it gave just enough room for a vehicle to bounce down it. After a short distance the thorn hedgerows petered out, leaving open views across fields and towards the rear of Prior's Farm. I pulled up in a gateway.

To the naked eye, the detail was indistinct. Only the chief features of the farmhouse stood out on the far side of the paddock. I could also discern the outline of a car, presumably the Fiat, parked alongside a rear wall, half hidden by trees. There was little else to be seen.

It was from here, I surmised, that Sandra would have taken her photographs. She would have had no need to get closer; her camera was a modern one, well up to the demands of range and focus. I sat thinking for a few moments. Then I reversed the Land-Rover perilously back to the lane and headed for home.

CHAPTER 13

The TV news that evening was presented by a young man with hair that seemed to have come out of a jelly mould and teeth that had evidently been designed for a face much larger than his own. The incisors were powerfully in evidence as he recounted the latest developments in the Elaine Turner murder hunt.

Links, he informed us, had been traced between the dead woman and certain shadier elements of the London gambling fraternity. Police were working on the theory that this might have some connection with her demise. I waited tautly for some reference to myself. The nearest he got was to mention, with a subtle inflection, that 'Miss Turner's possible associations in the Hampshire village that she had made her home' were likewise under scrutiny. Elaine, I thought, in her twisted way would have seen the joke. The regional news supplanted the national bulletin, and I went out to the kitchen to fry an egg.

A phrase or two, this time uttered by a female presenter, took me back into the living-room. The screen was now showing the inside of an air terminal. A tall, alpaca-swathed, platinum-haired man with a briefcase under his arm was approaching camera; he gave it a friendly grin as the disembodied voice of an interviewer asked whether he had enjoyed his trip to the UK.

'Had myself a great time. Been catching up on old haunts, good friendships . . . A week of pure nostalgia, I guess you'd call it.'

'You lived here for quite a while, of course, before returning to the States?'

'That's right. Place called Bobdean Manor, down there

in Hampshire, maybe you know it? A dozen or so of the happiest years of my life.'

'But aside from nostalgia, Mr Allanheim, your main purpose in coming back was to clinch a deal, I understand. Can you tell us something about that?'

'Sure. As you may know, I run a chain of stores back there in California, where I believe there's considerable interest—mounting interest—in certain of the foodstuffs England has to offer. Pastoral England, I'm talking about . . .'

'Organic products?'

'Well, sure, partly. I figure I know a little about them. During my time here, I acquired a taste for the local products . . . oh, let's see. Country-style fruitcake. Cheese scones. Preserves of various kinds.' Mr Allanheim's grin broadened. 'You could say I'm a sucker for all of that.'

'So you intend to introduce some of these food items into your own shops in the States?'

'That's about the size of it. Those lines we can import direct, we shall. The perishables we'll produce ourselves, to the traditional recipes, under licence. It's a good deal for us, and I hope it's a good deal for the folk down there in Hampshire who helped make my life happy when I lived among them.'

'You think the project will take off?'

'We'll be promoting it in a sizeable way.' He tapped the briefcase. 'I've one or two ideas inside of here; we'll see how they go. Thank *you*. My pleasure.'

Mr Allanheim's valedictory beam into the lens was blotted out by the returning visage of the presenter, a youthful blonde with startled eyes. 'A bit of Olde Englande, American-style,' was her pay-off line, before moving on to a round-up of regional road casualties. I flicked her out of the room. Returning to the kitchen to rescue the fried egg, I pondered this latest coincidence.

Assuming, of course, that it was coincidence. This seemed irrefutable. Angela's abrupt interest in a picture of Bobdean Manor could have no conceivable bearing upon what I had just seen and heard. On the face of it, it was simply one more instance of hearing something mentioned and then, within hours, hearing it again, after a lapse of years. Just the same, the juxtaposition of events was intriguing.

I liked the look of Mr Allanheim. He had that special American aura of businessman/philanthropist, steeped in homespun goodwill. For his sake as well as Hampshire's, I hoped the Californians stampeded for organically-produced Victoria plum jam in a big way.

The fried egg was a disaster. Settling for coffee and biscuits, I ate and drank while listening to a Bruckner symphony on the radio. At the end of it I felt sleepy, so I put my head back, observing the tidal flow across the ceiling created by the flicker from the electric fire. Conversational fragments from the recent past hopped around in my brain. There was sense to be made from them, if only I knew how to gather them up. Echoes of the music mingled with the phrases, clouding their effect. Thinking became something of an effort. I tried blanking out my mind, focusing on the psychedelic ripples overhead.

Presently I noticed an interference with the pattern.

It was not unlike the trickling of one shade of wet paint into another. A few seconds after becoming aware of it, I turned my head sharply.

The window facing the side garden was uncurtained. I was accustomed to the occasional shaft of travelling light that came from a vehicle's headlamps as it took the bend in the lane. This time, however, the entire window frame was illuminated. A dark shape seemed to hover at the back of it. I sat staring. Action of some kind was obviously demanded, but the lock that had been clamped on my limbs ruled that out for the moment. It occurred to me that I was, in fact, asleep, dreaming the manifestation. To jerk myself awake, I took a firmer grip of the chair-arms.

As if in response to the movement, the thing outside hopped aside, leaving the frame in darkness. I was barely on my feet when I heard the crash.

A pattering sound followed instantly. It was like heavy raindrops striking a metallic surface. When I reached the kitchen, the noise made by my feet—luckily I was wearing thick-soled trainers—sounded more like the scrunch of frozen snow. I was treading on a carpet of glass shards. Through the outer door, draughts from the garden whistled about my ears. Diving for the handle, I tripped over something and took a header beneath the breakfast bar. From outside, the clatter of footfalls down the path was followed by the slam of the gate; and then silence.

Hauling myself up, I wrenched open the door and ran in pursuit. The front of the cottage showed no sign of disturbance. The lane stretched away invisibly and inscrutably in both directions. Descending the steps, I made an arbitrary choice and wheeled to the right, trotted blindly for a few yards before hearing flapping sounds ahead of me in the darkness. They were almost upon me. Instinctively I raised both arms.

My left wrist was seized and held. The shock of contact made me grunt. A voice squealed in my ear.

'Paul? Don, it's Paul. I told you I heard something.'

Relieved but furious, I detached my wrist from Myrtle's grasp. 'I've just been attacked,' I said shakily. 'Did you see anyone?'

Light explored my face. From behind the torch, Don Jones was peering at me as though about to launch his own assault with a power drill. 'We just come out,' he explained. 'Left the dog asleep. Myrtle felt like a breath of air, so . . . Attacked, you say?'

'I told Don, I'm sure I heard something. Who was it attacked you?'

'What did you hear, exactly?'

'A sort of crash. We—'

'My kitchen door, that was. Somebody smashed the glass. Did you hear someone running off?'

'We heard someone running,' ventured Myrtle, 'but obviously that was you. The very next second—'

'Whoever it was,' I said resignedly, 'is nicely clear by now, that's for sure. I'll go back and clear up the mess.'

'Let us give you a hand . . .'

'Don't bother, thanks.' My reply sounded ungracious, as it was meant to. I was fed up with the Joneses. 'I'm learning how to cope with disruption,' I added tartly. 'Incidentally, if you must shift my tub to get at the manhole, I wish you'd put it back afterwards. It's intended as ornamental camouflage.'

'Tub?'

'On top of the inspection cover down there,' I said, indicating the side lane. 'Patty had to put it back for me.'

'We've not touched it. Have we, Don?'

'Not us, chum. We don't interfere with things that—'

'OK, forget it.' I didn't believe them, but I no longer cared. 'Maybe it was mutant rabbits. I'll be seeing you. 'Night.'

'We wouldn't do anything to . . .' Myrtle's voice pursued me mournfully as I made my way back, trying to devise a means of never having to speak to them again. Short of moving out, there seemed no possibility of this; and I was in no position to move out. I was trapped by debt and circumstances. Inside the kitchen, I found amid the shattered glass a brick-sized chunk of concrete which had made a dent in the wall plaster and rebounded to the centre of the floor, where it tripped me up again as I re-entered. Back on my feet and with my stock of invective nearing depletion,

I worked off steam with the aid of a broom, a bucket, and a dustpan and brush; after that I groped my way to the end of the garden and found in the workshop a sheet of chipboard left there by the builders who had, after a fashion, renovated the cottage. Staggering back with it, I nailed it over the gap in the kitchen door. By then it was eleven-thirty. I debated whether to go to bed. If it was going to be one of those nights, my head would only have to touch the pillow to trigger off more pandemonium downstairs. On the other hand, if I tried to doze in the armchair . . .

I went upstairs to bed.

The gaunt young man who came into the shop midway through the next morning proclaimed himself as Neil Barrett of the *Southern Reporter*. I asked to see his card. After a struggle with his pockets he found one, which I studied doggedly to give myself time to think. Finally I handed it back.

'A *Reporter* reporter?'

His thin lips widened dutifully. 'Right. Got anything to say to us, Mr Hunt, apropos the Elaine Turner case?'

My explanation that anything I might want to say would inevitably be couched in words of one syllable, unsuitable for publication in a family newspaper, left him seemingly unmoved. 'What we had in mind,' he suggested, 'was a reaction-piece.'

'A which?'

'How it feels to be, y'know, at the hub of a murder inquiry. Having to prove your innocence.'

'I can tell you that in a brief, well-known phrase or saying.'

Whipping out a handkerchief he mopped at his nose, which was prominent, inflamed and unstable. 'I mean, it's an experience, isn't it? One that not too many people are likely to have themselves. Generally, what we find, our readers have a fascination for—'

'No, they don't.'

'Pardon?'

'People can't have a fascination for things. It's things that have a fascination for people.'

He stared at me blankly, then gave up. 'You can leave the wording to me. How did you feel when you found yourself involved?'

'I can tell you how I'm feeling right now. Tired and overstressed. In no mood for the investigative Press. So would you mind getting out of my shop?'

He glanced around. 'I'm told you had a spot of bother here, too. Anything to say on that?'

'Don't tempt me. Are you leaving or not?'

'The publicity,' he remarked, 'could help you. *Man in Death Drama Hits Back*. You never know: someone reading about it might come forward with new information. It happens.'

Feigning absorption with the till controls, I thought swiftly while he attended to his nose again. I said, 'On the murder incident itself, I've nothing to say. The media have done it proud already. But there are one or two other things you might like to know—recent occurrences that make me feel I'm being victimized. Interested?'

Barrett dumped a tape-recorder on the counter between us. 'Shoot,' he invited.

After he had gone I had second thoughts. It was too late to summon him back. A telephone call to his office would, I suspected, be futile. Regardless of any retraction I could offer, the story was now his, to be exploited as he pleased. Somebody else came into the shop, and I wished it had happened sooner; an early interruption of the interview might have brought me to my senses. But the lean and hungry Barrett had been lucky enough to hit upon a slack period, and the damage was done. Cursing myself, I stood up to receive the newcomer. It was Sandra, looking pink.

'Hi there,' I said, doing my best to sound normal. 'You look upset. Something wrong?'

'Far from it,' she said tightly. 'You know what? Angela called yesterday.'

'To buy another picture?'

'She wanted a dozen.'

I gaped at her. 'You're joking.'

'Well, eleven more. With the Manor, a round dozen in all. Practically my entire stock.'

'All at half price?'

'Top whack for each. Over four hundred quid, the lot.'

'She must have money to chuck about,' I said faintly.

'So have we, now.'

'That wasn't meant the way it sounded. Obviously she has a first-class appreciation of art.' Rounding the counter, I planted a congratulatory kiss on Sandra's receptive cheek. 'Coffee and doughnuts,' I suggested, 'on the house.'

'Can't stop. John's expecting me back. I only sprinted along to tell you the good news and to give you this.' She planted something in my palm. It was a wad of five-pound notes. 'Your cut,' she explained. 'You've earned it.'

'I can't accept this. We agreed on ten per cent if I flogged any from here . . .'

'What difference does it make? Besides, with any luck you might soon be selling those as well.'

'Angela still in quest of more?'

'She didn't say . . . though it's a possibility, I suppose. Actually it's someone else.'

'Let me guess. Roger Ashby?'

'How did you know? Oh of course, he's a friend of yours, isn't he? Well, he rang me last night, asked if he could call in at the studio and see if there was anything he fancied. What do you think of that?'

'I'm not sure,' I said slowly. 'He'll be unlucky, won't he? You've hardly got anything left.'

'A few odds and ends. Early stuff that he might go for. Then there are the three that you've got here. I told him about those and he said he'd take another look at them after he'd been to the studio.' Sandra consulted her wrist-watch. 'He's due about now. Must dash. I'll be in touch. Isn't it exciting?' She rushed out of the shop.

Gillian emerged from the kitchen with a tray of fairy cakes. 'What's got her all worked up?'

'A career landmark,' I said, leaving her to fathom it out. I had plenty of my own to think about, including this latest development. What, I wondered, were Angela and Ashby up to, between them?

CHAPTER 14

Statuesque at her crazed porcelain sink, Bridget was rinsing vast quantities of spring greens with powerful thrusts of both arms. She welcomed me with a neighing sound. 'On your way home, dear boy? Lovely to see you. Stay for supper.'

'Thanks, I can't. The Chief Inspector wants to see me.'

'*Again?*'

'He's calling in at seven.'

'He must be potty. Phwat more does he think you can tell him?'

'I'll let you know. The reason I stopped by . . .' I passed a hand over my eyes. 'I've forgotten.'

'I'm not in the least surprised,' Bridget said severely. 'Have something to drink, at any rate. Help you unwind. I hear you've been raided again.'

'What?'

'Your kitchen window.'

'Oh—yes. How did you hear?'

'Myrtle called round for her eggs, and she—'

'I should have known. Did she sound uptight?'

'Uptight?' Laughter honked from Bridget's formidable stomach and larynx. 'What's she got to be tense about? Nothing she likes more than a slice of domestic drama.'

'I think I was a bit hard on her last night. Both of them. I suppose I should apologize.'

'Myrtle,' pronounced Bridget, restraining me with a hand as if to prevent me darting off immediately to throw myself at my neighbours' feet, 'is completely in her element and there's no need to suck up to her. Apart from your distressing experience, she'd something else to thrill her today.'

'What was that?'

'The sewage men turned up.'

'Thank God. Maybe it'll get her off my back for a couple of weeks.'

'Patty had a word with them.'

'The cesspool emptiers?'

'Yes. He happened to be coming up your side lane with Reggie and noticed they'd got the inspection cover up at the foot of your bank. He stopped to tell them it wasn't the right place, but they said they'd been told to clear the road drains as well, while they were here. Apparently they were choked with leaves from last autumn.'

'That's good,' I said absently. 'I won't stop for a drink, Bridget. Say hello to Patty for me, and I'll see you—'

'Wait a bit. There was a message for you.' Bridget scowled into her memory. 'They said to ask you, did you know there was a cable leading down the bank to the inspection chamber?'

'A cable?'

'With a rubberized plug attached.' Bridget bared her

immense teeth in a manifestation of risibility combined with disbelief. 'They seemed to think it was *most* odd.'

'Leading down from where?'

'Your garden, apparently. The men were too polite to investigate, not wanting to intrude: but they did wonder if you knew about it and whether it ought to be there. So Patty promised to pass the inquiry on.'

I stood frowning at the spring greens, stuffed into a colander like foliage outgrowing a hanging basket. Presently I received a painful nudge from Bridget's meaty elbow. 'Hullo? Anybody there? Any reply to my communication?'

'Sorry. I was just . . . I'm finding it hard to concentrate. Things seem to pile up. Thank Patty for me, will you, Bridget? I'll have a look for myself.'

The sewage men had been right. There was a cable.

Snaking down from the lip of the mini-embankment between my garden and the side lane, for most of its length the insulated wire was concealed by the jungle of grass and weed that I had allowed to rampage over the slope. At lane level, the flex terminated in a two-pin plug wrapped in plastic, stowed inside a crevice just behind the brickwork of the inspection cover. To a casual glance, it would have been no more than an item of litter that had added itself to the man-made detritus of the countryside.

Traced upwards, the cable took me to the fence at the top of the bank, where it tunnelled beneath a panel directly opposite the workshop.

Here, too, it culminated in a plug. In this case, it was of the three-pin variety appropriate to the cottage's electrical circuit. The final few yards had been left coiled around a nail projecting from the workshop's rear end, hidden from the approach path. This plug also was polythene-encased.

I stood there for a while in reflection.

A glance at my watch got me moving again. Returning

along the path to the kitchen, I swallowed a cup of tea and
ate a couple of buttered cracker biscuits while examining
the late edition of the *Southern Reporter* that I had brought
home with me. After our pre-lunch interview, Neil Barrett
had not sat around wasting his day. I could guess why he
had never contrived to put on weight. Most of his facts were
only slightly distorted and he wrote punchily, exploiting a
neat line in metaphor. I was scanning the piece for the third
time when a car's engine approached and died in the lane
outside. With a sigh, I went to the gate to meet the Chief
Inspector, who was shadowed by his sergeant, a taciturn
man with the unsuitable name of Milton.

'You're a minute late,' I told them.

'Newspaper article I wanted to finish,' Duke explained,
following me back to the kitchen. 'I see you've been opening
your soul to the Press.'

'I thought it wouldn't do any harm to give my side of
things.' Inside the living-room I waved them into chairs.
Sergeant Milton seated himself silently, notepad in hand,
close to the door. The Chief Inspector arranged his tape-
recorder on the table. I looked from one to the other.

'You seem determined I'm not to be misquoted.'

'If you were, you'd be the first to complain.' Duke flicked
his device into operation. 'You probably will anyway. Anything further to tell us, Mr Hunt?'

'I was hoping you might have something to tell me.'

'Like, we've traced six men with bloodstained cuffs, seen
in the region of Prior's Farm on the morning of the murder?
We're still looking.' He jabbed a thumb towards the
kitchen. 'What happened to your door?'

'A chunk of cement.'

'Careless of somebody. When did that occur?'

'Last night. But you wouldn't be interested.'

'Try me. Accident, was it? Do it yourself?'

'Naturally. I enjoy fixing chipboard over gaps at dead of
night.'

'Nab the culprit? Too bad. You are in the wars.'

'I'm getting battle-hardened.'

'So I infer. According to today's *Reporter* story, you've
been hit lately by a non-stop flood of mishaps, not forgetting
noise pollution, the vandalism of your shop, and now—'
he swapped expressionless looks with the sergeant—'wilful
damage to your domestic premises by persons unknown.
Whatever became of the village idyll?'

'Couldn't tell you. Any theories?'

'One could speculate.' He sat back. 'For example, one
could venture the opinion that a run of experiences of this
nature transcends ordinary bad luck. One might almost
detect a pattern.'

I captured his gaze. 'Based on what?'

He shrugged. 'A wish to divert suspicion. To appear to
be a victim of circumstance.'

'You seriously believe I'd put myself through all this, in
the hope of somehow fogging the issue, covering my tracks?'

'Barmier things have been tried. I remember a case—'

'I'm not interested in your archives, Chief Inspector.
What concerns me is here and now. If you've valid questions to put, put them. Or else leave me alone.'

'You must appreciate—'

'All I ask is a respite from wild accusations that make no
kind of sense. I'm sick of them.'

From the door, the faint rustling sound of Sergeant Milton changing the position of his knees interfered minimally
with the silence of the room.

Presently Duke coughed. 'The validity or otherwise of
my line of questioning, Mr Hunt, is for me to decide. In
actual fact, we're going to a deal of trouble over you. I
could have charged you long since.'

'So you've mentioned.'

'The fact that I haven't is not to be taken as implying I'm convinced of your innocence. An element of doubt exists, that's all.'

'Doubt, Chief Inspector? In *your* mind?'

'I may have views of my own on the matter,' he said calmly. 'That doesn't prevent me wanting to substantiate them.'

'In case the evidence falls down in court?'

'Any police investigator would be an idiot to run the risk,' he agreed with candour. 'This is why I'm giving you every chance to come up with counter-testimony that we can work on. So far, I'm bound to say, you've not produced much.'

'Well, I'm truly sorry. I've not had a lot of practice. The bits and pieces I do contribute—see today's *Reporter*—are blandly dismissed by you as a smokescreen, so what's the use? Finding positive leads to the killer is your job, not mine.'

'We're still after that mystery vehicle.'

'Good for you. Any pointers?'

'None whatsoever.'

'Am I meant to achieve a better result?'

'You've had several days to think. If you could let us have a list—a comprehensive run-down of Elaine's circle of contacts when she was living in—'

'How can I? I knew nothing of her crowd when I was . . . seeing her. After we split I lost touch with her—for good, I thought—and moved down here. So how could I possibly have any idea who she was consorting with?'

Duke folded his arms with an air of finality. 'You see our problem, then?'

'I . . .'

My brain ran dry. I sat staring at the blank face of the TV, half-expecting it to come out with a suggestion or two of its own. After another prolonged silence, Duke stood up.

'With the aid of our London colleagues, we'll soldier on for a bit. Should inspiration pounce, you know where to find me.' He paused at the door. 'You will bear in mind, Mr Hunt, that time's getting a little short?'

When they had gone, I went upstairs and changed into trainers, corduroys, two thick sweaters and a zip-jacket. Into a leather carrier I stuffed a heavy rubber torch with some life in it, a pair of thick gloves, a chocolate bar and a bottle of water. Downstairs, I drew the curtains across the front window of the living-room and left the lights on. Locking the kitchen door behind me, I took the path back to the workshop.

Visibility would have been enhanced by the quarter-moon, had it not been hidden most of the time by clouds windborne across the sky that gave a dry chill to the atmosphere. Inside with the door shut, the workshop was anything but draught-proof. The workbench was of solid construction. Stretching myself along it, I rested my head on the carrier, having first put on the gloves and positioned the torch against my right thigh. Then I settled down to wait.

Within twenty minutes I was stiffer than the boards holding me up. Nailheads that had not existed when I lay down had begun to carry out drilling operations into my flesh. Air currents penetrated me like needles applied by an unskilled acupuncturist. Rattles came from the door. After an hour I was ready to give up, hobble back to the cottage to switch on every heating appliance I possessed. Obstinacy held me to the bench, like a vice-gripped plank ready for planing.

I nibbled at the chocolate, wishing I had had the sense to bring a Thermos flask and sandwiches. Each time I took cautious aim with the torchlight on my wrist, I hoped to find that I had dozed for a couple of hours and it was now midnight; on each occasion it wasn't. By ten, every muscle in my body was screaming. My bone structure was set in permafrost. If it became necessary to move . . .

Above the gusts and the rattles, a new sound reached me.

I sat up. When it came to the point, movement posed no problem. The noise had come from outside: a high-pitched scrape, like a metal stud on a flagstone. As I rose, the torch rolled perilously close to the bench edge. Grabbing it back, I swung both legs to the floor, watching the door.

It continued to judder. Up to now, the wind had been responsible; now there was a difference. The oscillation of the woodwork had a more deliberate cadence, as though an animal were butting it with its head. I shifted my fingers to the base of the torch. Its fat weight was a comfort.

The door started to open.

Before I could activate the torch, the moon escaped briefly from the clouds to silhouette the shape in the doorway. All I could see was an outline. For a moment we stood, the two of us, frozen in tableau, and then the shape backed off. I heard the sound of an impact against the fence.

I was slow in pursuit. Bodily numbness held me back at the fence; by the time I was over, my quarry was down the bank and into the side lane, pounding towards the dip. When I started to run, the bones in my feet raised protests. For the first few strides they snapped and cracked with agonizing unexpectedness, nearly pitching me over. After that they worked themselves looser and I was able to pick up the pace.

The moonlight had lasted only seconds. The side lane was in darkness; I was navigating from memory. Although there was a real possibility of drifting off course into disaster, my mood was to abandon caution: this was a chance I was determined not to miss. I allowed the downhill gradient to take me over. At the foot of the dip, where the lane curved twice before launching its ascent on the other side,

I was going at full gallop, spurred by the fact that the footfalls ahead seemed to be moving back on me. Uphill, I began to toil. But the moon was out again and my pupils were adapting to the conditions. Now I could see the figure ahead. It was labouring. I summoned up some spare breath.

'Come here, you!'

Unsurprisingly, the request was ignored. The outcome, however, was not affected by this idiotic appeal to reason: I was gaining fast and the figure was tottering. Presently it tripped.

Thrown to its left, it took a header into the gully that flanked the roadway, creating a viscous splash which shot pellets of stinging moisture into my eyes. Blinking them away, I dived across the verge to seize the pair of booted feet that remained within reach. One of them kicked out feebly. With my forearm I locked both heels. Before long they went passive.

'Had enough?' I inquired of the feet.

The reply that came from the submerged end consisted of a gasp, a choke and a cough. Accepting this as acquiescence, I commenced to haul.

The shape slid back slowly, spitting fragments like a firework expiring on a wet night. When fully back upon the verge, it turned on its side to hack painfully into the long grass. Alert to a possible ruse, I waited for the paroxysms to subside.

When they showed signs of doing so I turned him on to his back. The maleness of my victim was now beyond dispute, even though hanks of drenched hair obliterated most of his face. Tweaking them aside, I gazed down into a pair of bulging eyes.

''Evening, Kevin,' I said. 'Expecting to find me at home, were you?''

CHAPTER 15

'So you know who it was?'

Slamming the range door, Gillian scrambled upright to confront me. 'All them noises an' that? Your kitchen winder? The break-in we 'ad here?'

I nodded. 'The culprit for the lot.'

'Anyone I know?'

'The gentleman in question,' I said carefully, 'would certainly be familiar to you, but there I'm afraid we must leave it. I doubt if he'll be doing anything of the sort again.'

'Oh, you are rotten. Why can't you tell us?'

'Sorry, Gill, I promised. He's learned his lesson . . . I think. There's no way you'll worm it out of me,' I added as her mouth reopened. 'It wouldn't serve any purpose; not now. With any luck I shall be left in peace from now on, at least from that quarter. Can you do me another small favour?'

'Seeing it's you, Mr Hunt,' she said forgivingly. 'But I still think—'

'Least said,' I intoned, 'soonest forgotten. I have to pop out for twenty minutes. Can you stand by here, as ever?'

'Off to see the constable, are you?'

'A competitor,' I smiled.

At the entrance to Lionel's showroom I paused. The slight delay wasn't necessary, but it gave me a moment of keen satisfaction: I knew that he had been aware of my approach across the street. When I did thrust open the door, Lionel was being hyperactive at the back, rearranging nests of inlaid coffee tables with his meagre backside pointed my way. The temptation was great. Standing off,

I surveyed his activities. Presently I coughed. With an exaggerated jerk he leapt back, spun daintily.

'Paul, dear boy! How you do creep up on one. In the nicest way, I mean, of course. And how is life treating you?'

'Less cryptically, thanks, Lionel.'

'*Really?* That does sound intriguing. You mean, they've a line on the ladykiller? I do hope so. Let me take that out of your way . . . The *clutter* in here. Some refreshment, dear boy?'

'I'm here on business.'

His pale blue eyes peeped out at me. 'Don't tell me, Paul, you've come to *buy* something?'

'No. To offer my congratulations.'

He blinked rapidly, four or five times. 'Have I won something?'

'I think you've just lost. But I must commend you on the effort that went into your bid. Nobody could have tried harder.'

Lionel stepped cautiously out of the coffee tables to adopt a hands-on-hips attitude before me, his vivid green suede jacket gracefully apart like classical theatre curtains to place on full display the high-buttoned, coral-pink fluted shirt he was wearing underneath. 'My *bid?* I'm not with you, dear boy.'

'That I've finally come to realize. You've been against me all along.'

'Now really. You mustn't—'

'An intruder. An interloper. A main street marauder.'

'What?'

'Isn't that how you saw me? Why you were willing to go to such lengths?'

He dabbed a conciliatory paw in my direction. 'You've had an awfully hard time, Paul, just lately. It's natural you should look around for scapegoats. But you know, you're being frightfully unfair. You really shouldn't come storming in here, hurling accusations which—'

'Last night,' I interrupted pleasantly, 'I had a little talk with someone. Quite a chat, in fact. Highly informative. Tied up any number of puzzling loose ends. I wonder if you can guess who I was speaking to?'

He pulled elaborate faces suggestive of mental delving. 'Someone to do with the police?'

'No; with the land. Young Kevin Riley.'

'Who?'

'Come on, Lionel. Everyone knows Kevin. You do, certainly. He has your fingerprints on his bankroll to prove it.'

Lionel began to bluster. 'This really is too bizarre. Bankroll? Fingerprints? Now that I think of it, Kevin works for Cyril Blake, doesn't he? How did he come into this?'

'Quite readily, I gather. He's a young fellow with expensive hobbies and he's in debt to his eyeballs. That is, he was.'

'I honestly don't—'

'Unless he could lay his hands on some quick cash, Kevin faced having all that electronic gear of his repossessed. To say nothing of anything else he owned. No disco equipment; no transport. A shattered lifestyle.'

'I fail to see—'

'Then suddenly, a lifeline. What should come up for grabs but the Felrose Bursary?'

'I can't even begin to imagine—'

'No imagination required, Lionel. You wanted someone to do your grubby work for you: Kevin was more than available. All it took was a chance conversation one lunchtime at the Stag.'

Unthinkingly I took a pace forward. Lionel hopped backward, as if confronted by a rampant stag in the rutting season.

'Relax,' I said kindly. 'Some of us avoid the rough stuff,

where possible. When was it, Lionel, this conversation? Soon after Christmas? The time when you came to tot up your profits for the year and found they weren't up to much . . . or convinced yourself they should have been fatter. And who was to blame? Why, that nasty newcomer Paul Hunt opposite: who else?'

'You have my solemn assurance—'

'Gone was your monopoly of morning coffee and afternoon teas. Everybody drifting over to the Pantiles instead. Fearful dents in your balance sheet. Dire need for action.'

'Whatever Kevin's been telling you—'

'Has the ring of truth about it, you'll be alarmed to hear. The road accident, the shop break-in, the concrete lump through the window . . . Kevin's production methods might have been his own, but your greasy trademark was stamped on everything. You came up with the ideas, he carried them out.'

'That's absolute—'

'Afterwards, money changed hands. I actually saw it happen on one occasion, quite by chance. When transacting deals at night, Lionel, you really should switch off the lights. You're a bit exposed to the street from here.'

'I've nothing to—'

'Hide? That's a matter of opinion. What's for sure is that it was profitable for Kevin and a good investment for you, because you couldn't see me toughing out of that sort of harassment for long. Sooner or later, by your reckoning, I was bound to chuck in the sponge, get the hell out of the village, back to where I'd come from.'

Tears had started to dampen Lionel's optical region in a somewhat repellent way. 'You were never meant to come to any harm,' he wept. 'The accident was a mistake. He was meant to just crumple your vehicle, shake you up a bit.'

'Sorry I was thoughtless enough to drive over the escarpment instead. Some people just won't cooperate, will they?'

'Kevin was—'

The showroom door opened behind me. Dabbing at his eyes with a lace-fringed handkerchief plucked from his breast pocket, Lionel hurried past me with bared teeth. 'Mrs Philpott, how *lovely* to see you back. You've called about the dresser? I've had the handles replaced, totally in period, and it's now with the french polishers who hope to be finished by Friday. So if you like, we can arrange . . .'

I let him get on with it while I ran an eye over his bogus merchandise. As far as I could judge, the shop was a monument to commercial chicanery, which in the circumstances seemed not inapt. On the eventual departure of Mrs Philpott he crawled back to me like a puppy braced for a slap on the nose. 'One of my *three* customers this week,' he said piteously, carrying out further remedial work on his eye sockets. 'Trade really has slumped, you know, Paul. If I hadn't been frantic with worry—'

'I'd never have learned all about sound augmentation in ducted channels, domestic bliss for the ruination of. That's one thing I owe you, Lionel. Kevin was most explanatory. My education in electronic wizardry is almost complete.'

'That was *his* idea.'

'But I'm sure it must have appealed to you. A heavily-amplified tape of sound-effects played inside a drain inspection chamber, so that the noise ran up the pipe into the space under the floorboards . . . pure genius. No, really. I'm lost in admiration.'

'Kevin told me—'

'And to use the victim's own power-source for the purpose: that was the final deft touch. Full marks.'

'We just thought it would give you some sleepless nights.'

'Shall I tell you, Lionel, what brings on insomnia with me? The thought that there are slugs like you oozing up from the wet grass, eager to cause damage. But for that, I'd sleep a lot sounder.'

He wrung his hands. 'What are you going to *do*, Paul? What are you going to *say*?'

I eyed him with contempt. 'Do? Nothing. And all I want to say, strictly between the two of us, is: cut it out. Lift one more manicured finger to make my life a misery and I'll shop you to the world. Lay off, and we can continue to co-exist . . . just. Is it a deal?'

'Oh Paul. I don't deserve this. You're too charitable. I don't—'

'You're right: you deserve something altogether different. But with all my other problems, I simply can't be bothered. I've told Kevin the same thing. As long as he jacks it in, we can forget about it. Nobody else need ever know. That's all I came across to say. Good morning to you. And a prosperous summer to both of us.'

As I made for the door, he cantered around the far side of his floor display to intercept. He clutched at my sleeve. 'Wait just a moment, Paul. I want to make it up to you. I'm sure there must be something . . . I want things to be right between us. I hate to think of you bearing a grudge.'

'Perish the thought.' I disengaged my wrist. 'Get this into your skull, Lionel. Stay out of my hair and things between us will be nothing but sweetness and light. Just don't come within five yards of that pavement over there, OK?'

He sniffed like an infant. 'I wish you wouldn't speak like that. If there's anything I abhor, it's unpleasantness. Look here, Paul, these other problems you mentioned. If there's any way I can help . . .'

'There isn't. Forget it.'

A look of desolation spread over his face. 'You're a great chum of Sandra Millett, aren't you? She seemed a little upset yesterday.'

I turned back. 'Upset? What about?'

'To do with some photos,' he said eagerly, 'that had gone missing. I overheard her talking to the checkout girl in the supermarket. She sounded quite perturbed.'

'More likely the prices that were bothering her.'

'I believe not.' Lionel wriggled. 'Why not have a word with her, Paul, ask if there's any way you can help? She might be . . . grateful.'

'Thank you,' I said coldly, 'for the advice. I'm sure if Sandra's in any trouble, she'll seek aid from the best quarter. She has other chums, besides me.'

Gillian greeted my return with surprise. 'Thought you was going to be longer than that. Bill Coker rang. He'll be making a delivery about eleven.'

'Fine. Any other messages?'

'Oh, there was another call. From Sandra Millett. Said she'd like a word with you, if you can spare a minute.'

'Did she say what it was about?'

'No. She sounded a bit het up. I said you'd ring her back.'

When Sandra answered she was tight-voiced. 'Sorry to disturb you in shop hours, Paul, but it's rather urgent in a way. No, nothing to do with John. I'd like to talk to you, but I don't want to say it over the phone or at the shop. You couldn't possibly look in here at lunch-time?'

'I'm expecting a delivery at eleven. I'll come along straight after. Now what's troubling her, I wonder?' I remarked to Gillian, dropping the receiver. 'She should be feeling on top of the world.'

'Photos,' announced Gillian with an air of inspiration.

'Explain.'

'She's lost some. My cousin was telling us, she come into the supermarket all in a tizzy yesterday because they'd gone missing, like. Relies on her snaps, doesn't she?'

'How can you mislay a set of prints? Don't attempt to

answer that. I'll try to find out at midday. In the meantime, Gill, I want you to promise me something.'

'Yes, Mr Hunt?' She hung on my words.

'If that creep from across the road even looks like mincing this way, give me an early warning and head him off, will you?'

'Count on me,' she said with grim satisfaction. 'What's he done—tried to fleece you?'

'You could put it like that.'

The first customer of the morning was Ashby's wife Sally, smart in a two-piece tweedy suit and high boots, her hair newly permed. 'By myself this morning,' she explained, taking the initial bite out of a slice of buttered toast. 'Roger's doing the property rounds, you'll be amazed to hear. He feels now might be a good time to buy. The market seems to be bottoming out.'

I said casually, 'Got his eye on anything in particular?'

'Some barn, I think he mentioned. I never know quite what he's up to. To be perfectly frank, I sometimes wonder if he's up to anything, to speak of. He just enjoys nosing around.'

'I have to admit, I can't remember the last time he actually bought anything.'

'That hovel in Judd Lane,' Sally said promptly, 'down by the timber mill. Not exactly a coup. He finally resold it at a loss. I wouldn't call him a business prodigy, exactly. But then, it keeps him occupied, and we don't need the money. I've plenty from what my father left me. We're very lucky.'

'Please don't mention fathers, just now,' I implored.

'Why not?'

'I'm feeling guilty about mine. I still owe him money.'

'You'll pay him back. Doing quite well here, aren't you?'

'I was just starting to break surface. Then a few minor distractions came along.'

She gave me sympathetic appraisal. 'Yes: you've had some rotten luck. Still involved with the police?'

'I'm the Grade A suspect,' I reminded her, 'and shall be until they trace the real culprit . . . which could take us well into the autumn, on current progress.'

'It'll work out, you'll see. You've another customer, from the sound of it.'

The new arrival was Bill Coker, the delivery man from Roffman's, my main supplier. I helped him in with the goods, then fed him a few of the doughnuts left over from the day before and waited while he consumed three beakers of tea and recounted the sad tale of his wife's arthritis. When he had finally driven off, I told Gillian that I was going for an early lunch and would release her for the afternoon when I came back.

'You've done more than your fair share lately. Take a trip to the coast. Tomorrow you'll feel a new girl.'

'Reely, Mr Hunt, you don't have to—'

'No argument. You've earned a break. If the Chief Inspector or anyone else wants to interview me again, they'll have to come here to the shop.'

I walked the half-mile to Sandra's home. It was a bright but chilly day, and when Sandra came to the door she was wearing a bright smile that also seemed to be doing its best to hide other elements. 'Come in, Paul. Hope this isn't too much of a drag for you. John thinks I'm making a fuss. Say hallo to him and then we'll go up to the studio. Stay for lunch?'

'Can't. I'm relieving Gillian. Hi, John. I hear you're coming Big Brother.'

He chucked his chin. 'Sandra has a tendency to panic. Must be the artistic temperament. Good hunting.'

Sandra was waiting for me by the trestle table in the studio. 'Don't tell me—he said I was over-reacting? It's all right for him: he doesn't have to make a living from bits of celluloid. Oh, I wish he could, poor dear. But what I mean is, for me it's serious. If I can't find that film, I'll have to waste any amount of time going round all over again, taking more pictures.' She thrust fingers through her hair. 'Sorry —I haven't explained, have I?'

'I gather some prints have gone astray?'

'Vanished. I can't think what's become of them.'

I glanced around the studio. 'Where do you normally keep them?'

'Here, on the table.' She pointed. 'And the negs in that top drawer, over there.'

'Can't you have fresh prints made from those?'

'They're missing too.'

I looked at her. 'That does seem peculiar. You're quite sure?'

Hurrying across to the scarred oak chest in a corner, she pulled out all three of its drawers. 'See for yourself. That's where they should be, in folders on the right-hand side. All gone.'

I rummaged vainly with my fingers. 'You don't have anyone in to clean?'

'That'll be the day. They'd charge the earth. Anyhow I wouldn't want someone poking around, disarranging things. Nobody comes up here except me. At least . . .'

She hesitated. I sent her a look of inquiry. 'Someone did,' she said with reluctance. 'The day before yesterday.'

'Who?'

'Mr Ashby. You know I told you he wanted to see what other work I had available? Well, I showed him what there was, which didn't add up to much. There's the Prior's Farm thing—' she nodded towards the easel—'which he wasn't much interested in; and then the only other thing of any size is that rough outline of the Old Barn at Lower Denning, which I plan to paint next. The photos of that are among those that are missing.'

I sat on the chest of drawers. 'When did you realize they'd gone?'

'Not till yesterday. After Mr Ashby left I had to attend to John, who was having one of his bad days, and I couldn't get back to the studio until yesterday morning. That's when I missed the prints.'

'While Mr Ashby was up here,' I said with deliberation, 'did you have occasion to leave him and go downstairs?'

Sandra flushed. 'Yes, I did. Just for a few moments. John was calling out. He'd got a foot trapped under his wheelchair, somehow. I went down and extricated it and came straight back.'

'So Mr Ashby was in here by himself?'

'Only for a minute.'

'Long enough, apparently.' Rising, I slid the top drawer experimentally in and out. It ran almost noiselessly. I gave Sandra a meaningful look which she returned with more than a touch of embarrassment.

'You think Mr Ashby took them?'

'Seems the only explanation, doesn't it?'

'But why?'

'That's asking. The Old Barn at Lower Denning . . . Is that up for sale, do you happen to know?'

Sandra looked mystified. 'Yes, it is. At least, there was a board up when I was there a week ago, taking shots. It's on offer for conversion, with twelve acres including a lake . . . it had all the details, with the name of the agent. What does that have to do with—'

'Search me, but I'll bet there's a connection. Roger's pretty interested in old property, as you probably know. I think he may be on to something.'

'But why should he need my photos?'

'I don't know.' I stood dissecting my thoughts. 'This sudden interest in your pictures seems to have arisen since a conversation he had with Angela in the Stag. She got in first with her mass purchase, and now it's as if he's afraid of missing out on something. Question is, what is it?'

Sandra gazed at me with a mixture of hope and bafflement. 'If it was Mr Ashby, why would he take the negatives as well?'

'Good question. Want me to try and find out?'

'*Could* you? I was hoping you might offer. I don't like to ask him myself. It seems such a nerve, especially if we're wrong; I might wreck my chances of more sales. I know he's a friend of yours. I thought perhaps—'

'Leave it with me.' I gave the drawer a decisive final shove. 'I'll see what I can do.'

'By the way,' she said as we went downstairs. 'I do have one solitary print left. One of the half-dozen I've been working from.'

'Prior's Farm?'

'Yes. I happened to notice something about it the other evening—well, it was John who spotted it, actually. We thought you might be interested, so I put it aside to show you. What with one thing and another, I'm afraid I forgot all about it till now. Let me show you. John, where did I put that photograph?'

'In the bookcase. The others are probably there, too,' added her brother, giving me a wry look. 'If not, you took them down to the Oxfam shop with the *Reader's Digests*.'

'I shall ignore that. Here we are,' said Sandra, handing me the print. 'This is what John noticed.' She positioned a forefinger to show me. 'See?'

I held it up to the light. 'You bet I see. How very interesting.'

'That piece of foliage rather gets in the way, but John reckons an expert analyst . . . They have high-powered equipment, don't they, for scanning?'

'Aerial surveillance,' John said with authority. 'They can

interpret virtually anything from that. Why not the same from ground level?'

'Why not, indeed?' I felt the stirrings of excitement as I continued to study the photograph. 'May I keep this for a while? I've a feeling that a certain Chief Inspector of my acquaintance might be fairly interested to see it himself.'

CHAPTER 16

On my way back to the Pantiles I was tooted by a passing Mercedes. It braked ahead of me and Ashby's face peered from the driver's window.

'Any developments?' he called.

I crossed the road to the car. 'What with?'

'The murder, you clown. What else?'

'There is something else, in point of fact. You're just the guy I wanted to see.' I squinted at his digital clock on the dash panel. 'Got a few minutes for a quick one at the Stag?'

'I'm due over at Riverfield. Now that you mention it, though, I do feel thirsty and a bit peckish. Good idea. Hop in.'

'I was planning to give you a buzz,' I said as we drove the few hundred yards to the inn.

'Oh? What about?'

'A matter of some delicacy.'

He flipped me a look. 'Sounds appetizing. Let's have it.'

'Wait till we get inside. I'll order while you're parking. What will you have?'

'The usual, and one of those burger things with some farmhouse fries. Been chasing around this morning. Hope the place isn't crowded to the rafters.'

On the contrary, the lounge bar of the Stag was unpopulated apart from a lone, hunched figure in a corner. It was that of Lionel Felrose, brooding over a vermilion beverage in a tall glass. At my entry he half-started to his feet, thought better of it and relapsed into watchful humility. Disregarding him, I placed my order with the relief bar-tender—Rosemary had lunch-times off—before selecting a table as remote from Lionel's as was consistent with the room's geometry, to be joined presently by Ashby with a spring in his stride.

'This mine, old son? Cheers. Food on its way? Great. What did you want to see me about?'

'Sandra Millett.'

He blinked. 'Young Sandra? What's her problem? I thought you said she was on the verge of breaking into the big time.'

'So she might be, if she can retrieve her stock-in-trade.'

Ashby took a gulp of Scotch. 'Why, what's she lost?'

'The photos she works from. They're essential to her.'

'Shouldn't lose track of 'em, then, should she?'

I sat looking at him until he glanced back. 'She's pretty sure they've not just been mislaid, Roger. She rather thinks you swiped them.'

His brown eyes acquired a wounded expression. 'What an accusation! I could have her for that.'

'Possibly: but did you?'

'Would I do such a thing?'

'If the stakes were high enough,' I said bluntly, 'you'd do it without a quiver. And the evidence points strongly your way.'

He drank again, put his tumbler down, sat staring at it. 'What's your involvement?'

'Unofficially I'm Sandra's agent. I'm acting as go-between.'

'Oh, I see. And there was I, deluding myself that we were buddies. I never took you for—'

'It's because we're pals, Roger, that I feel able to be

frank. I'd appreciate some candour in return. A lot hangs on this. If you did take Sandra's prints and negs, there must have been a compelling reason—at least from where you're standing. In that case, I'd like to hear it.'

His gaze wandered. Meeting the gimlet eye of Lionel, fixed upon the pair of us with the intensity of a dog imploring a titbit, he returned it hurriedly to me. 'Why do I get the feeling you've made a damn good guess already?'

'I might have an inkling.'

'And you're asking me to pencil in the detail? Tall order, isn't it?'

'Is it?'

'You must know it is.' He sat pondering me, his drink evidently forgotten. From the counter, the bartender said tersely, 'Burger 'n' chips.'

'I'll get it.' I went over for the plate, paid for it, asked for salt. On my return, Ashby was looking as if he had reached a decision.

'Otherwise,' he resumed, 'you wouldn't be asking, would you? If you see what I mean. You're *expecting* evasion. Well, my son, that's hardly my style. When a thing's partly in the open, why not drag out the rest, give it some air?'

'OK. Start dragging.'

'Not here.'

'Why not?'

'Walls have ears, etcetera. Drink up and come outside to the car.'

'What about your lunch?'

'Someone else can have it. I've lost my appetite.'

Suddenly he looked tense. Finishing his drink in one swallow, he waited while I did the same before getting up and making for the exit. Conscious of Lionel's continued scrutiny, I followed him out. Releasing the doors of the Mercedes with a jab of a remote control, Ashby installed himself at the wheel and waited for me to join him. 'What do I owe you for the meal?'

'Never mind. Time's getting short.' I was thinking of Gillian, awaiting her afternoon off. 'I want to hear what you have to say.'

He fired the engine. 'I'll just stooge around a bit while we're talking.' Easing the vehicle out of the car park, he picked up speed out of the village. Luxury padding embraced me. I fingered the fascia.

'Very swish. Brand new?'

'Picked it up a few days ago,' he said complacently.

'Traded in the Carlton? Property speculation must be booming.'

'I wouldn't say that.' With an open road ahead, he piled on the acceleration, sliding me a wink. 'There are times, my boy, when the best investment consists of a well-heeled spouse. Smooths out life's little tucks and creases.'

'If I didn't know you better, I might have said that was a pretty cynical view of Sally's function. Where are we going?'

'Just round and about. You wanted me to come clean.'

'I'm waiting.'

'I wonder where I should start . . .' His fingers tapped the wheel. 'Difficult, isn't it? I suppose, basically, it comes back to that property speculation you just mentioned. The reason I was able to do something for the girl, in her hour of need, was my interest in local habitations. I knew the agents were having trouble finding a buyer. I figured they might jump at an offer to lease for six months, while the market picked up. Which they did. It wasn't until—'

'Hold on.' I turned in my seat to stare at him. 'Just who and what are we talking about?'

He frowned through the windscreen. 'Elaine, of course, and Prior's Farm. Who did you think?'

'I was under the impression . . . It doesn't matter. Go on.'

'You were under the impression . . . ?'

'Not important. Keep talking.'

He removed a hand from the wheel to finger his chin. 'Are we on the same waveband, Paul, you and me? I'd assumed we were. Now I'm less sure.'

'Try me.'

'If you insist.' A note of abstraction had entered his voice. 'To proceed, then. When I told Elaine I'd rented this farm on her behalf, she seemed actually quite grateful . . . until she saw it. Not exactly the type, is she, to be separated from the bright lights for long? At the best of times, Prior's Farm hardly ranks as a fun place. Small wonder she got twitchy.'

'How did you know she did?'

'I looked in a few times, to help keep her spirits up.'

'You said you hadn't been near the place.'

'Well, I would say that, wouldn't I? The precautions I took, you wouldn't believe. Didn't want Sal getting wind of it. She's easily hurt.'

'No point in upsetting your sole benefactor.'

'Exactly.' Ashby was beginning to sound more cheerful. 'So, timing my occasional visits to ensure privacy, I did what I could for Elaine's morale, told her to sweat it out until the heat was off. The last time—'

'I never quite twigged why the heat was on her in the first place.'

'Are you kidding? That latest boyfriend of hers, Cashanti —bad news, he was, in anyone's language. She told me a thing or two about his goings-on. Not much, because she was obviously petrified at the thought of him.'

'When did they split up?'

'Can't give you a date. But the break-up was messy, I'm sure of that. Cashanti had already threatened her a number of times. Once they were apart, he was convinced she'd talk, expose his activities. Elaine knew this. She was literally in fear of her life.'

'I'd guessed that.'

'So anyway, that last time I called in at the farm, she was doubly uptight because she'd heard on the radio that Cashanti was facing tax charges. As a potential witness, she was scared he'd put in an extra effort to trace her, wipe her off the map. I did what I could, made a few soothing noises, but I didn't stay long. I wasn't easy about being there in daylight. I'd parked my car round the back, as usual, next to hers, but—'

'What day was this?'

'The day of the murder.' Ashby shook his head sadly. 'As I drove off, I remember thinking I was taking a risk by bringing the car into the yard at all. I decided to park further away in future, then walk down from the lane. Only it never came to that.'

I stretched my legs. The warmth of the car was starting to get to me; I felt drowsy, and yet at the same time curiously alert. 'Elaine's death made you a possible suspect?'

'Well, you see, I wasn't sure if I might have left traces. Fingerprints. Footmarks. Tyre patterns in the mud. I was in a cold sweat for a few days.'

'I think I know the feeling.'

Ashby gave a snort over the wheel. 'You had my sympathy, of course, when the cops started leaning on you; but I assumed the Cashanti link would soon emerge. I thought there'd be an arrest in no time.'

'The professionals make it harder for the police than that.'

'Then I heard they were looking for a car. That gave me a jolt. I was pretty sure nobody had spotted me driving into the farm that morning, but . . . I just had to hope for the best. And take what action I could.'

'Change cars?'

He nodded. 'Just as a precaution, I traded the Carlton in for this job, using a dealer some distance away. If the police had really got stuck in, of course, the Carlton could soon have been traced to me, but short of that . . . Then I heard something else.'

'You heard,' I said sleepily, 'from a helpful guy called Paul Hunt, that Sandra Millett had been at Prior's that very morning, with a camera.'

'Right. And that set the alarm bells jangling again. What if any of her shots included the Carlton? It was just feasible that she was clicking away while I was there. I couldn't be certain. So I had to find out.'

'You made an excuse to visit Sandra's studio and pinch the lot.'

'And it's as well I did. One of those prints,' Ashby said dramatically, 'showed a view of the farmhouse taken from the back, across the paddock. And next to Elaine's Fiat you could just see a glimpse of the back of my car — complete with number plate.'

'You can read the number?'

'Not with the naked eye. But with all their state-of-the-art technology, I'm sure the cops would soon have had a few questions to put to me.'

'They sure would.'

'Which is why I held on to the prints *and* negs. Actually I've destroyed them. I'm sorry about Sandra. But it's hardly a catastrophe for her; she can take some more. My priority was me, I'm afraid. All clear now?'

'Reasonably.' I struggled into a more upright posture, trying to shake the cottonwool out of my head. 'You knew Elaine, then, back in London?'

'Some while before you did, old son.' He despatched another wink. 'Between ourselves, we were having quite a fling at one time. All highly discreet, it goes without saying. And well and truly over,' he added piously, 'before you came into the picture, and before Sal and I moved here. I never imagined our paths would cross again.'

'But when Elaine split with Cashanti . . .'

'And started feeling menaced, I was the guy she came to for help. She knew I dealt in property. She thought I could find a place round here for her to go to ground.'

'She was right, wasn't she?' I heaved my train of thought back on track. 'Though I don't see why you should have felt under any obligation, if things were over between you.'

'Old times' sake, old boy. Recognition of past services rendered.'

'Who served whom, I wonder? There's one thing puzzles me . . .'

'Mm?'

'When you left the farm that morning—the day Elaine was killed—how did you get your car past my Land-Rover? I left it blocking the gateway, I thought.'

'You did. But the keys were still in it. I managed to—'

Ashby broke off.

Correcting a slight swerve off course, he remained silent for a moment before speaking again, more softly.

'That was smart, Paul my son. Quite smart indeed. How did I fall for that one?'

Ahead lay a left turn. At the last second, Ashby veered into it, wrestled for control of the Mercedes, regained the centre of the lane and picked up speed. I held on to both armrests, my head swimming.

'Where are you making for?'

'Back to the village.'

'This won't take us. It was you, wasn't it? You're the one who clobbered me on your way out.'

He said nothing.

'Then planted the clock in my wagon. Having first made sure my prints were on it. You moved the Land-Rover to get your car past, then shifted it back. You hoped I'd take the rap.'

His left hand made a gesture. 'All's fair in lust and self-protection.'

'So it seems. Elaine getting demanding, was she? Something of an embarrassment?'

'If you really must know,' he said after a pause, 'Elaine was being Elaine in block capitals . . . a condition you probably know all about. You were right, of course, just now. Our affair wasn't over. I never could shake the damn woman out of my system. And once installed at Prior's, she had me over a barrel and she knew it.'

'She threatened to tell Sally about the relationship?'

'Elaine wasn't one to miss a trick like that. Knowing how I felt about Sal—'

'Just how do you feel?'

'I'm very fond of her.'

'Not her cash, of course? The assets that let you lead the kind of life you want to. Endless free time, luxury cars, tours of properties on the pretext of dealing in them . . . Early retirement with a gold lining. You'd hate to have to give it all up. You've grown accustomed to the pace.'

He shrugged. 'Think what you like. You're right: I couldn't have Elaine blowing the gaff and wrecking everything. To keep her quiet, I paid her those visits at the farm I mentioned earlier . . . but again, you've hit it, she did get demanding.'

'What happened?'

'On that last occasion, she said she'd contact Sal and tell her everything unless I gave her . . . oh, I don't know, some astronomical sum to enable her to get abroad, start a new life out of harm's way. Quite an attractive proposition, in its way. Except that I hadn't anything like the amount she was asking.'

'You could have got it from Sally.'

'Only by pretending it was for a property deal . . . and then, when no deal transpired, she'd have got suspicious. Anyhow, I made Elaine an offer. She just laughed. We were up in her bedroom. I tried to make her see the problem, but she didn't want to know.'

'Elaine,' I mumbled, 'was hardly the understanding type.'

'In the end I got frantic. She told me she had this mobile phone in her wardrobe—I don't know if she had or not—and she was going to call Sal there and then unless I coughed up. I couldn't let that happen. I grabbed her as she got off the bed. She started struggling like a maniac. Spitting, clawing . . . I couldn't hold her. I clutched the first thing that came to hand . . .'

'The clock.'

'I only meant to knock her back with it. I must have swung it harder than I intended. There was this ghastly noise: next thing I knew, I was staring down at a lot of blood . . .'

Although he was gripping the wheel, Ashby was allowing the nearside tyres of the Mercedes to maraud over the ruts and tussocks of the verge. I felt too sleepy to be scared. I said with a certain limp pomposity, 'Hard to live with, a thing like that.'

'Oh, you get used to it. Don't fool yourself, young Paul. The only reason I'm spitting it all out is to fill in what would otherwise be a pregnant silence between now and our arrival.'

'Arrival where?' I queried thickly.

'You'll see.'

'Drive back to the village. No point in . . .'

'Why don't you sit quietly and nod off? That's what you'd really prefer to do, if I'm not mistaken.'

CHAPTER 17

When I awoke, the darkness was encamped on me.

Although I seemed to be lying on straw, the layer was thin, allowing the chill of the stone floor beneath it to seep into me. For a moment I fancied I was back inside the workshop, trying to prevent my muscles from seizing up. Movement brought a yelp out of me. A more cautious attempt took me into a sitting posture from which I reached out tentatively with an arm. My fingertips touched something.

It felt like a rough wooden surface, vertical and unyielding. Maybe I *was* back in the workshop. By leaning forward, I was able to use the edge of the woodwork as a support.

I came groggily to my feet.

Memory stirred. Echoes of the voice of Ashby. *Swung it harder than I intended* . . . It was as though he was there, within reach of me. So powerful was the impression that I called out.

'Roger? Is that you?'

My voice added to the resonant effects. I felt a little nauseous. Guiding myself by the plank, I took a few tottering paces to my left before coming up against stone-work. Using this as a boundary line, I steered myself along until the texture of the stone gave place once more to timber. Leaning my weight against it, I felt the faintest of tremors. I dealt it a thump.

Slight vibrancy and a set of barked knuckles were the result. The door, if it was one, ranked among the more solid of its breed; furthermore, it was set so flush into its frame that not a chink of light gained entry. Unless it was dark outside. I wished I could see the hands of my watch.

If it was dark, I had been there some hours. The dryness of my throat supported the conjecture. I tried to estimate what time we had arrived.

Hazily, I recalled being helped out of the car. Ashby's hand under my elbow. My own mumbling. I hadn't wanted to mumble: the formation of words was a challenge I couldn't meet. I felt like a drunk. On a single Scotch and soda?

The bed of straw as it came up to hit me was the last thing I remembered. That and the slam of the door, retreating footsteps. How many hours ago was that?

Groping my way on, I completed the circuit of the room, or whatever constituted my surroundings. At the cost of a jarred kneecap as it struck a projection, I regained my original spot, gripped the plank again, stood pondering. The sick feeling was starting to ebb. My brain felt sharper.

Items clicked into place.

Lower Denning. The words on the signpost as we swerved left into the side lane. In my fuddled state I had half-registered the name; now it was Sandra's voice that came back to me. *The Old Barn at Lower Denning, which I plan to paint next.* Up for sale. A snip for a speculator. Earlier in the day, Ashby had been out and around, visiting likely properties. Including the Old Barn? In which event, he could well have been given a key . . .

Something interfered with my train of thought.

No sooner had I identified it as the throb of a car's engine than it cut out. For a moment, silence trickled back. Then I heard them again: the footsteps. Brisk, incisive, as they had been when they went away.

There was no time to feel around for loose implements.

Approaching the door, the footfalls halted, to be replaced by metallic clattering sounds. Belatedly setting off across the floor towards them, I had taken only a few paces when Ashby's voice floated in from outside.

'Awake, Paul?'

The inquiry was low-pitched but distinct. Resumption of human contact came as a vast relief. I came to a halt. 'You bet I am. Where the hell have you been?'

'Stand away from the door. Unless you want a cartridge through your guts.'

The greeting sounded less than affable. I sprang to my right, stretching out vainly for something to grasp. A final rattle preceded the draught of air which indicated that the door had opened, although I could still see nothing. Suddenly light glared into my eyes.

Shutting them, I turned my face away. When I looked back, he was leaning against the doorframe, aiming the torchglow at something he was holding.

'See this? It's rather lethal. So I want you to come forward nice and slowly, keeping both hands where I can see them. That's fine. Follow me out.'

The toe of my right shoe jagged slightly on the ribbed concrete outside. Ashby swayed clear. I couldn't make out his features, but I knew he was watching me intently.

I said, 'I don't know what you think you're playing at, but we can't—'

'Shut up. Walk forward. Follow the torchlight.'

The ground sloped downhill. From concrete, the surface changed to rough turf, a little spongy, difficult to traverse in the darkness even with the aid of the torch. It descended some distance.

I felt an urge to resume discussion with Ashby as he followed up. There was much that I wanted to ask him. Something told me, however, that when requesting silence, he meant it. Expecting to reach the car, I felt my stomach pitch as the turf under my feet became firmer, funnelled into a track of pebbles which in turn led to a structure that looked like a gangplank. It stretched out over water. The torchlight probed and darted.

'Go along to the end.'

'Look, Roger, isn't it time we stopped playing games? Isn't this all a bit childish?'

'I stopped playing games some hours ago.'

My heart joined my stomach at low altitude, leaving only blind instinct as a motivating force. I considered pleading with him. Even this ultimate humiliation was beyond reach: I could think of no way in which to couch an entreaty.

Boards rang under my shoes. The jetty rocked a little. There was no handrail. The platform went out about fifteen yards, covering the shallows of what was evidently a lake, of uncertain extent; the torchbeam illuminated a fair expanse, but the opposite shore was out of sight.

A thought exploded in my brain. Where there was a jetty, there was usually a boat. If there was, it would be moored at the end. Feeling better, I went on almost eagerly to the termination of the planks.

Looking down, I could see only water.

No boat.

The woodwork quivered as Ashby advanced nearly to my elbow. His voice was completely matter-of-fact.

'Sorry about this, Paul, but I've no choice. Tough luck on you, but that's the way it goes. 'Bye, old son.'

From the corner of an eye I caught the movement of his arms.

Duck, I instructed myself. Dodge; sidestep; *do something*. Paralysis had taken a grip. The boards beneath me were swaying, like trick flooring at a fairground. There was a hammering in my ears.

My eyelids, I noticed, had started to blink uncontrollably, as if to pre-empt pain.

I stood waiting for it to happen.

A kind of gasp came from Ashby. Maybe, I thought dully, the shotgun was too heavy for him. Wielding a thing like that . . . He gasped again, then swore. A confusion of noise came from behind me.

My limbs unlocked. Turning, I peered into haloes of light, half-blocked by grappling figures. Ashby seemed to be struggling in the grasp of an octopus. A voice, not his, came out of the gloom.

'OK, Mr Hunt, we've got him. You can step away from the edge.'

'You're a lucky bloke,' announced Chief Inspector Duke in the car going back.

I glowered at him. 'If that's the case, I don't think I want to be around when they're dishing out the misfortune, if you don't mind.'

'I meant lucky,' he said mildly, 'in the sense that your abduction didn't go unobserved. There's something to be said for small-town curiosity, after all's said and done.'

'Who was it who was curious and observant enough to notice?'

'Mate of yours, I understand. The gentleman who keeps the curios and bric-à-brac in the shop facing yours.'

My mouth fell open. '*Not* Lionel Felrose?'

'That's the name. Seems he was in the Stag enjoying a lunch-time drink when you and Ashby came in. He saw you talking and was a bit struck by the manner of the pair of you. So he was watching rather closely when you went to the bar to collect a plate of food, and . . . Tell me, Mr Hunt. Did you find yourself coming over muzzy a short while after that?'

'It came on in the car. I could have slept for a week.'

'Hardly surprising. Mr Felrose says he saw Ashby slip at least four tablets out of a small bottle into your Scotch while your back was turned.'

'So that was it.' I threw my mind back. 'Ashby used to

pick up sleeping tablets for his wife. He must have had some on him.'

'How convenient. Well, Mr Felrose didn't know quite what to do about it. He was going to come over and say something, but then almost immediately the two of you left. Through a window, he saw you get into the Mercedes and take off. He took a note of the number.'

'Dear old Lionel,' I said, almost fondly. 'Ever my best interests at heart. How did you know I'd been taken to the Old Barn?'

'Nobody did, at that time. All that was known was that you'd gone missing. Your young lady at the shop—'

'Gill? Kicked up a fuss, did she?'

'All she kept saying was, "Mr Hunt wouldn't have stopped off when he said he was coming back." By three o'clock she'd reported you missing. And I don't mind telling you, it set off alarm bells all over the place.'

'Why?'

Through the semi-darkness of the car I detected a quirk of the Chief Inspector's mouth, an upward twist of his left eyebrow. 'Why? It may have slipped your mind, Mr Hunt, but until then you occupied top spot on our list of suspects, remember? The thought did cross our minds that you might have decided to, ah, discontinue cooperation with our inquiries and fade into the mist. Which would have meant very red faces all round, with mine as the beacon.'

'I hadn't seen it from that angle.'

'What else was I supposed to think? Incidentally, what exactly was it that prompted Ashby to slip you the sleeping pills? He realized you'd rumbled him?'

'At the time, I hadn't. He just assumed I had. All I intended was to tax him with the removal of Sandra Millett's photos, thinking he wanted them in connection with some dubious property deal he was hatching. He thought I'd guessed the real reason for his taking them, and so—'

'You had to be silenced. Well, luckily, the moment he heard you were missing, Mr Felrose had the gumption to come through with an account of what he'd seen, plus make of car and number. That gave us something to look for.'

'Took you a while, didn't it, to track him down?'

Duke withered me with a glance. 'We did have quite a few hundred possible square miles to cover. Ashby's wife wasn't much help. All she could tell us was, her husband had said he'd be out all day, viewing property. So it was hard to know where to start.'

'You tried the estate agents?'

'That did occur to us,' he said crushingly. 'After the fourth one, the trail ran cold. It seems Ashby had looked in during the late morning—just before running into you, that would have been—to pick up some printed details and mention that he was going on to Riverfield; only he never got there. None of the Riverfield agents had clapped eyes on him. And yet he was somewhere, all afternoon and most of the evening—somewhere away from the Barn. You were there by yourself, sleeping off his tablets.'

'He must have taken cover until dark.'

'Obviously. And then made his way back via his home, to pick up the shotgun. If his wife was watching TV or something, she may not even have seen him. After that he drove on back towards the Barn . . . and that's where his luck ran out. He was spotted.'

'Who by?'

'One of our patrols,' Duke said smugly. 'Following orders, they didn't flag him down: tailed him instead. We hoped he might lead us to wherever you were.'

'Good thinking,' I applauded.

'They do say I'm not just a homely face. Mind you—' the Chief Inspector hissed faintly—'we'd no intention of making it such a cliffhanger. But he couldn't be chased right up to the Barn itself, you see.'

'Why not?'

'If he'd had headlamps blazing into him from behind, he might have panicked and done something stupid. He was armed, don't forget. Not that we knew that, but we had to take the possibility into account. So our blokes abandoned their vehicle outside the Barn grounds and followed on foot.'

'Having first radioed for help?'

'Naturally. By the time we all bowled up and made it to the Barn door, he'd got you down to the jetty and was in the act of flexing his wrists with a view to assisting you headfirst into the lake. Our intervention was a bit last-minute, for which I apologize.'

'Think nothing of it.'

'But it did have the effect of driving the final nail into the case we've now got against him.'

'I'm glad of that.' I thought for a moment. 'His idea, I take it, was to make it appear I'd put an end to myself?'

'Tormented by guilt and calamity,' Duke nodded. 'No longer able to cope with it all.'

'But to make sure I drowned, he was going to bash me senseless with the shotgun first. Wouldn't that injury have aroused suspicion?'

'Not necessarily. In falling, you could have struck your head on the end of the jetty, or a stone on the lake bed. Alternatively, one of Cashanti's mob might have been assumed to be responsible. There'd have been nothing in particular to associate Ashby with any of it.'

'Except . . .' I felt in an inside pocket. 'Maybe this.'

I held out Sandra's surviving print. He peered myopically. 'Can't see. What is it?'

'A shot of Prior's Farm, taken from the rear by Sandra Millett on the morning of the murder. Under a good light, you can make out part of Ashby's previous car, a Vauxhall

Carlton. It was parked next to Elaine's while he was inside the farmhouse with her.'

'Holy smoke!'

'He was afraid there might be a print showing that—and when he had a chance to look through them, he found he was right. What he didn't know was that there were *two* similar shots. This is the one Sandra and her brother noticed, so she kept it aside and gave it to me this morning. Ashby wasn't aware of that. He thought he'd collared all the evidence.'

'We'll have it examined,' Duke said with evil satisfaction, pocketing the print. 'Time we're through, we'll get him done for every crime committed in the area in the past three months. No, I musn't get carried away. One killing and an attempt is more than enough to be going on with.'

He was silent for a space. 'It's his wife,' he added suddenly, 'I feel sorry for. Seems a nice woman.'

I put my head back with a groan. 'As always,' I said, 'it's the innocent who suffer.'

AFTERTASTE

'We've two ducklings from the freezer,' Patty assured us, banking the fire with wet logs, 'so there should be ample and to spare. You've all brought appetites along with you?'

The three of us exchanged looks. Angela said heroically, 'I can never say no to poultry.'

'You can resist anything, except temptation?' Having collected the customary acknowledgement of his favourite gem, our host returned his attention to the fire-basket, which was sending up volumes of dark grey smoke accompanied by spitting noises. He gave it a few unproductive jabs with the nearest implement to hand, which was a toasting fork, before leaving the mass to smoulder while he explored the sideboard. 'Dry sherry, Sandra, or medium?'

'Medium, thanks, Mr Sheeney.'

'Patty to my pals. I'm afraid there's no medium. No dry, come to that.' Bottles went flying. 'Here we are . . . cream sherry, will that do? No, I'm sorry, that's empty.' He looked round with tragic eyes. 'A glass of white wine?'

'That'll do nicely.' Sandra gave him a beaming smile. 'I don't care what it is, as long as we celebrate.'

Bridget appeared from the scullery. 'I've not heard everything yet. Phwat's it all about? Who's this Carl Aluminium?'

'Allanheim,' Angela corrected her gently. 'He's the American stores magnate who had Bobdean Manor for a number of years.'

'*Him.*' Bridget gave a toss of the head. 'We always knew him as Midwest Bill, honorary Lord of the Manor. So what is it he's doing — publishing a book?'

'He's having a publicity brochure produced,' Angela

explained patiently. 'It's to go on display in all his outlets,
advertising this range of English country foodstuffs he's
putting on sale.'

'I see,' Bridget said blankly.

'It's all going to be done on a lavish scale. Descriptions
of Hampshire village life, which I'm going to write, illus-
trated by colour plates of typical rural buildings . . . which
is where Sandra comes in.' She smiled across at the girl.

'Hey,' I said. 'You should do that more often.'

The smile faded. 'Do what?'

'That muscular facial extension you've just demolished.
I'd barely seen it before.'

'I smile if there's something to smile about. You'd go
along with that, wouldn't you, Patty?'

'Certainly. When I was living in Bantry Bay—'

'Pipe down, you old bumbler. Angela's talking.'

'As soon as I heard,' the schoolteacher continued, giving
Patty an apologetic glance, 'that Mr Allanheim was on the
scrounge for suitable pictures, I immediately thought of
Sandra. Only I had to be quick. I knew he was flying back
to the States the following day and I wanted him to see a
sample of Sandra's work before he left. As it happened, I'd
been talking to someone the night before . . .'

'Roger Ashby?' I put in.

'Hah!' came explosively from Bridget. 'We don't mention
that blighter's name in this house any more, do we, Patty?
Cold-blooded villain. Phwat did you want to speak to *him*
for?'

'At the time,' Angela said humbly, 'I'd no more idea
than anyone else what he was like. He was quite fun to talk
to: seemed to know most of what was going on in the district. The subject of the break-in at Paul's shop came up,
and he mentioned that a few of Sandra's paintings had been
on show there. So next morning I rang to ask if they'd
survived. When I heard they had, I meant to go over to

take a look, but a string of crises cropped up at school and I couldn't get away. So that evening—'

'She invaded me at home,' I informed the others, 'and got the remains of Bobdean Manor for half price. I couldn't understand, then, what the urgency was.'

'It was the ideal sample,' Angela pointed out. 'The Manor had been Mr Allanheim's home for eleven years; he was deeply attached to it. And Sandra had captured it beautifully. I was sure he'd love it. So I grabbed it and ran.'

'Phwere to?' demanded Bridget.

'To Mr Allanheim's hotel in Kensington, where he'd been staying. I'd been there once already, because we're old acquaintances and he'd asked me to look him up. A few years ago,' she enlarged, seeing our perplexed faces, 'I gave special coaching to his granddaughter. She was behind with her reading, and while she was staying with the Allanheims at Bobdean he advertised for someone to put her through a crash course . . . which I did. And we got quite chummy.'

'When he saw the painting,' I said, 'he fell for it?'

'Hook, line and sinker. He wanted to see more, but he couldn't delay his return to the States because he'd urgent business to attend to. So he asked me to get hold of as many as I could and send them out to him. Hence—' Angela transmitted another smile — 'my subsequent raid on Sandra's reserves.'

'And there was I, thinking you'd been captivated by my sheer artistry.'

'I was,' Angela assured the girl. 'We all think your work is top-rate and worthy of a wider audience. Which is why I pulled out all the stops.'

'And my word,' breathed Bridget from the door, 'didn't it just pay off?'

'How much is he paying you, Sandra?' Being both ignorant of and indifferent to matters of finance, Patty was completely without inhibition in debating the topic. Sandra's response was in the same spirit.

'Five hundred per canvas. Except for the one of Bobdean Manor, which he wants to reframe and hang at his home outside Los Angeles. A thousand for that.'

'Pounds?' I inquired. 'Or bucks?'

'Sterling currency,' Angela said crisply.

'That's quite a heap of currency.' I made a quick calculation. 'Six and a half thousand. Terrific.'

'With the prospect of more to come. There'll be a royalty,' Angela explained, 'on every copy of the brochure they flog in the supermarkets. Could amount to quite a bit extra.'

'Plus,' appended Sandra with a bubble in her voice, 'it should get my work known in that part of the States, at least. Maybe an exhibition somewhere. Who knows?'

'In the meantime,' I said, 'you'd better start thinking about getting yourself turned into a limited company. And you'll be able to afford help to look after John. That'll give you more time to paint. Which, in turn—'

'It couldn't have happened to a nicer person.' Traversing the room, Patty inclined himself to plant a grave kiss on Sandra's left cheek. The girl laughed shakily.

'I still can't believe it *has* happened. I'm convinced I'm going to snap awake, any second.'

'Signed the contract yet?' I asked.

'It's just gone back. He'd signed already.'

'That's fine, then.'

'And I want you and Angela to share the commission.'

'Don't be daft. The money's all yours.'

'Angela gets ten per cent,' the girl said firmly. 'I want you to have five per cent as well, Paul. Without the two of you, I wouldn't be in the position I am.'

'Angela did the spadework. I'd nothing to do with it.'

'If you hadn't put my stuff on view in the first place, Angela wouldn't have known about it.'

'I agree with Sandra. But she's not paying you an extra five per cent, Paul. You must take half of my cut.'

'Don't be absurd.'

'What about that loan from your father? You said you were anxious to pay it back.'

'Of course, but—'

'If you're going to squabble among yourselves, children,' bayed Bridget, 'I'll be getting on with the lunch. Patty, top them up and get 'em all tipsy, that'll put a stop to their nonsense. Can anybody smell burning?'

'I can,' Patty said on a hollow note. 'That'll be the duck. You've got the oven set too high.'

'What's another lump of charred flesh,' his wife said blithely, 'after all that's been happening lately? If it's inedible, we can offer it to Lionel Felrose as a fossil. He might get a good offer.'

I buried my face. 'Please don't mention Lionel. In future I've got to be nice to the guy.'

'I should hope so. Can't be unfriendly with someone who helped save your life.'

'I can't? No, you're right, Bridget. I'll have to learn to co-exist. Hardest part is going to be persuading Gillian to accept him as a member of the human race. She loathes his guts.'

'The girl,' opined Patty, busy with bottles, 'has taste.'

'Patty, will you come and carve? The rest of you can sit down while I bring in the soup. And no arguments, you hear? This is a triumph, not an autopsy. Have you all made notes in your diaries?'

We looked at her in silence.

'My bring-and-buy,' she proclaimed, 'for the horses. It's next week. You'd not forgotten?'

We all made dissenting noises. When she and Patty had withdrawn purposefully to the scullery, I caught Angela's eye across the table. She was looking particularly schoolmarmish in a high-necked cardigan and with her face almost barren of make-up, her hair dragged back. I wondered why I needed to keep looking at her. Having captured her attention, I was obliged to think of something to say.

I said, 'Why don't we donate part of our commission to the horses?'

'Two per cent each,' she responded promptly. 'The rest can go towards our debts. You repay your dad: I'll reduce my mortgage. You approve, Sandra?'

'Have some fun with it as well.'

'All right,' I said. 'Tomorrow's Saturday. I'll buy Angela lunch at the coast and we can . . . discuss things. Are you on?'

She gave me one of her looks from the head of the classroom. 'What things?'

I scratched my head. 'How about the new cooker we're going to buy for Bridget, before she and Patty starve to death?'

The magenta face of our hostess appeared round the door. 'Sorry, you people,' she announced. 'The soup's burned as well. D'you mind sardine hors d'œuvres?'